EMBROILED
IN
WAR

DAN RAPP

This book is dedicated to my classmates, University of Notre Dame Class of 1959, who died in the service of our country.
- Dan Rapp

1ST Lt RICHARD S. HORSFALL, USMC - 02 NOV 1962

2ND Lt LEONARD J. LeROSE, USAF - 23 DEC 1963

Capt EDWIN G. SHANK JR., USAF - 24 MAR 1964

Capt JOHN G. BYRNE JR., USMCR - 02 MAR 1965

Capt JAMES J. CARROLL, USMC - 05 OCT 1966

Lt CURTIS R. BAKER USN, - 28 MAR 1967

Lt EUGENE M. VAICHULIS, USN - 30 SEPT 1968

Lt Col JAMES A. FOWLER, USAF - 06 JUNE 1972

Embroiled In War

ONE

AT A TOWN ONCE PEACEFUL

The small Belgian town had a name, but Sgt. Don Veator of Syracuse, New York didn't know it. What he did know was that a German SS panzer unit could be headed there and all he had was himself and twelve other men to stop it.

Don shielded his eyes from the glare of an overcast sky as he inspected the charges and wiring placed under the bridge. Although another unit had placed them, Don was satisfied that they were well placed and well hidden.

Climbing back up the river bank opposite the town, Don found the detonator box in a fox hole. Evergreen boughs hid the position from the view below. At his command post he could see the .50 caliber machine gun and the two bazooka team positions further down the embankment.

Everything was set that could be set, but he wished he had surveyed the positions from the opposite side of the river. "Too late now," he thought. Despite the freezing temperature, perspiration dampened his shirt. After opening his field coat he took a long swig from his canteen. Gazing down on the valley below he couldn't help but think how peaceful the town, the river and the bridge appeared, like a photo from National Geographic. A blanket of powdery snow added to the serenity. Calmly, he rearranged the evergreens in front of the fox hole, then slid into it.

At arm's length away crouched Dave McMillan straining to see any movement down stream and across the river. His 7x50 binoculars never left his eyes, "Do ya think they'll come this way, Sarge?"

"I'd be surprised if they didn't. This is the only steel structure bridge for miles around. Those old stone things might not stand the weight of a heavy tank."

McMillan's face wrinkled with concern, "Damn, and here we sit with a mighty force of thirteen guys and we're waiting for heavy tanks? Thirteen guys, like one from each of the thirteen original colonies ya might say."

"Ya might," responded Veator.

"Well, the colonist from Pennsylvania thinks we ought to blow the bridge and get outta here."

The binoculars were still fixed to McMillan's forehead, when Don replied, "The bridge is not to be blown unless the Krauts attempted a crossing. You know that."

"Yeah, yeah. I know it. I just don't like tangling with cuckoo SS people with fancy assault rifles, no less tanks."

A hundred feet away, Buzz Capra leaned out of his gun position waving his arms to get Don's attention. He then pointed to the right and downstream.

The road paralleled the river, ran through the town, and then took a left turn to the bridgehead. What Capra was gesturing about became audible in the roar of two motorcycles. Soon the riders could be seen as they flashed between the buildings. Helmets, goggles, and long leather great coats covered them as they made their turn to the bridge.

At the edge of the bridge, they dismounted. *Phutt, phutt,*

phutt, phutt. almost in unison, the engines continued to idle as if connected to the same ignition system.

Cautiously, the two cyclists descended the bank, one on either side of the bridge. Peering up, they scoured the underside just as Don Veator had done thirty minutes earlier. They seemed satisfied and then hustled back up the bank.

McMillan thought this enough reason and urged Don to blow the bridge, "Now, Sarge, now. Blast 'em."

"No, Mac, we don't know what's behind them," Don answered.

The motorcycles roared back from the direction they came. Five minutes later the cyclists were back, slower this time because of what trailed behind them. Engine noise and the clanking of tracks on the pavement preceded the visual contact of an armored car and two Mark IV tanks. "Reconnaissance in force," Don muttered under his breath.

The plot had thickened. No longer was blowing the bridge in doubt, only the timing was in doubt. Thirteen GI's watched intently from their hidden positions as an officer wearing a garrison cap and padded camouflage suit emerged from the armored car.

Down the embankment he went to see what the others had already seen. Obviously satisfied that the bridge was not wired, he returned to the road level. After waving the first tank to proceed, the officer walked slowly back towards his armored car.

The second tank, still at ninety degrees to the bridge, began to roll also. Once more Capra waved for Don's attention. With his index and little fingers, he was suggesting, "Get both tanks."

It did not take Don long to decide the issue. If only one span collapsed, he'd have a tank on the near side of the river, not a good deal. He shook his head "no" to Capra and then watched as the first tank clanked to the center of the first span.

With the detonator plunger firmly in hand, Don whispered, "That's far enough." *Zzzztt,* went the plunger. A series of muffled explosions ran along the right side of the bridge. A horrible groaning sound issued from the bridge as it tilted. Rivets popped from their holes like champagne corks. The bridge continued to tip, sending the tank sliding through the guard rail. The bridge spans and the tank hit the frigid waters of the Salm just as the bazooka teams loosed their rockets. Simultaneously two armor piercing, burning charges struck the second tank. It exploded a second later. Orange swirling flame leaped up through the open hatch. For an instant the tank commander sat motionless as the flames devoured him, then he slipped down and out of sight. Exploding ammunition inside the tank wrenched the turret from its moorings and sent it tumbling to the ground.

In the midst of the fireworks, Capra's .50 caliber gun joined the din. The familiar bark from its muzzle sent heavy slugs through the armored car's plates, through the engine block and through the gas tank. A column of black smoke shot up, followed by orange flame.

The volley did not come in bursts of four or five, but rather in a steady stream. Capra had no need to save ammo or barrel wear and worked the stream of shells over the motorcycles. Drivers and machines tumbled backwards from the impact of the high energy bullets.

Through the smoke and fire, two figures darted for the safety of the buildings back up the road. Small arms fire kicked at their heels until they reached the stone fence which jutted out from the first building.

"Cease fire," Veator shouted. "Let's get the hell out of here." He started to gather his things, but couldn't help looking at the carnage caused by the engineer squad turned weapons platoon. The bridge structure peaked out of the swiftly running water in five or six points, but the first tank was nowhere to be seen. The rest of the vehicles burned with columns of black smoke caught and tossed by the winter breeze.

From his gun position, Capra shouted, "Do we bring the

gun, Sarge?"

"Not unless you want to carry it. Bring the bolt mechanism though."

Speaking only to himself, Don added, "The last thing we want is for Gerry to turn that thing on us."

Dave McMillan gazed at the scene below just as Don Veator had done moments before. "Are we gonna get a medal or something for this, Sarge?"

Don disconnected the detonator wires. "Probably not. Do you see any officers here to send in a recommendation? I tell ya what. I'll buy you a beer the first chance I get."

"Deal," said Mac.

In March of 1945, Don Veator's 299th engineers' battalion crossed the Ludendorff Bridge at Remagen and into Germany. With liberated Deutschmark from a liberated bank, Don bought several barrels of beer and started a battalion pub. Dave McMillan got what was promised to him a hundred fold.

The contribution of the combat engineers in the Battle of the Bulge cannot be overstated. The entire German operation was intended to split the American and British armies and seize the Dutch ports. This plan could only succeed if a strict seventy-two hour time table could be met.

The German vanguard, headed by SS Obersturmbannfuhrer Joachim Peiper, was frustrated time after time by groups of American engineers who blew up the bridges he needed and disrupted his time table.

The actions at the Salm and Lienne Creek, a short distance away, stopped Kampfgruppe Peiper, forcing it to seek other crossings. All the while, it became vulnerable to fighter bomber attack and used up precious fuel supplies.

Details of "At a Town Once Peaceful" were not secured from military records or books, but were told to me personally by Don Veator himself, three years before his death. This author is proud to say that I knew him, if only too briefly, and like to think of him as a friend.

TWO

THE GUNS AND THE WINTER SKY

The barracks room was cold and dark when Cpl. Thaddeus "Ted" Zackiewicz lowered himself onto his bunk. With thirty-one missions and six pints of beer under his belt, he wasn't feeling any pain. He wasn't bad drunk, like after his twenty-fifth mission, but drunk nonetheless.

"Four more to go, he muttered to himself. "Just four more." For ten minutes Ted lay motionless, the blanket folded away from his shoulders. The winter night cooled his face and neck where the beer began to break through the pores.

Then, like a slow motion film in the movie theater, he began to replay the events of the day's mission. The Focke-Wolfe 190 came in on a half roll. "Bandits at eight o'clock," the intercom squawked. Like a duck on the wing back in Wisconsin, Ted tracked him, led him just enough to keep the tracers ahead. But no tracers flew, and his gun didn't go *blam, blam, blam, blam, blam*. Empty shells didn't rattle on the metal floor. "My gun's jammed. "Shit," he said as he pressed the triggers again. Continuing to swing the barrel, he pressed the triggers a third time to no avail. "Shit, shit, shit." Ted slapped the side of his .50

13

caliber.

Anger, despair, frustration surged through Ted as he pulled on the bolt. It didn't budge. Dropping to one knee, Ted stared intently at the bolt. The slot was surrounded with a misty layer of frost, like the stuff that forms on the corner of the windows on a winter day in Racine. Again he pulled the bolt. Grudgingly it moved, ejecting a live round to the floor. "About goddamn time," he barked into his mask.

The Focke-Wolfe with the yellow cowling and a modeled gray paint job was long gone. "Damn, I could'a pasted him. Three bursts easy," Ted said loudly. "I was right on his ass."

In the silence of the room, Ted began to picture something else. The enemy fighter was right on him too. Four cannons and two machine guns, but no flashes lit the wings. Better yet, no tracers found their way to his B-17, the "Darlin' Jean."

For a moment Ted's mind drifted. His pet peeve still gnawed at his gut - the nose art of the "Darlin' Jean." Whereas other ships had voluptuous girls in bathing suits or less, "Darlin' Jean" sported the head of a round, freckle faced female with red hair. She was more like one of the losers in the Sadie Hawkins Day Race than a pin up. "Why couldn't we have Daisy Mae or Moonbeam McSwine if we're going to Dogpatch for a girl?" The captain's wife or fiancée, or whoever she was, would have to go.

Then the Focke-Wolfe movie played again. Again no cannon flashes and no tracers flew at the "Darlin' Jean." Ted smiled broadly as he realized the Kraut pilot's guns jammed too. "*Ha, ha, ha.* Nature called a cease fire," he laughed. "Nature called a cessation of all hostilities. *Ha, ha, ha, ha.*"

From out of the darkness, a room mate asked, "What's so goddamn funny, Teddy?"

"Nature called the war off this afternoon. Isn't that a bitch?" His laughing only amplified as he pondered the bizarre event. His sides and shoulders shook. His stomach muscles tightened. Tears formed in his eyes, ran down his cheeks. "Nature called

14

off the fuckin' war. *Ha, ha, ha, ha."*

The voice from the dark was not amused, "We'll see how nature does Monday when we have to go back."

Several more ha-ha's followed as Ted's pent up emotion burned itself out. A moment of silence was followed by two more muted laughs which worked their way through Ted's mirth system. Then a longer silence prevailed as the beer worked on him, and sleep closed in. The blanket still laid folded back exposing his shoulders to the cold.

OOO

At the officers' mess near Nordhorn, Germany, Hauptman Bruno Hoelker squeezed the last few drops from a bottle of cognac. "Maybe the Amis won't come tomorrow," he thought. "The weather is closing in. I need a day off." The stress of flying combat and the cognac had taken a toll on Bruno. His eyelids drooped to half-mast.

With his boots propped on the table and his chair tilted back, Bruno thought about the butt chewing he'd just experienced. The JG kommander was usually a good sort but he was getting ridden from higher up. Every military man knows what the plumber knows - shit flows down hill, Bruno thought as he sipped. He had stood at attention, his cap under his arm and took it. "No victories in six missions, now seven. You are supposed to be a veteran pilot, an experienced fighter. How can you be a role model for these young pilots we are forced to use, when you yourself don't perform?"

The Luftwaffe grew weaker every day, while the Allies grew in number and quality of pilots and machines. The brass could not begin to realize the abnormal chances Bruno was taking. In an effort to get back on course, to get another victory, he had been reckless. Today's attack on the B-17 could have been disastrous.

After out foxing a swarm of P-51's to get a crack at the

15

bomber, he found himself with a dangerous approach angle. It may have been good for getting off a long burst, but it exposed him to the bomber's guns for too long. He had thought at the time, "I have to risk it. Who do they think they're dealing with? Seventeen victories, the knights cross - in any other country I would be a hero."

The "they" in his exasperation was not the American bombers, but the unrelenting brass. The expectations increased as the probability of losing the war became more apparent. "The Mustangs fill the sky and we're rationing C3 gasoline," Bruno muttered under his breath.

With his glass half full, Bruno swirled the amber fluid, took a deep sniff of the aroma. "Cognac should be enjoyed in peace time, not war." Then he sipped, swallowed, sipped again. As he brushed his fingers through his close cropped, blond hair, Bruno realized his fingers were trembling. At arms length, he could see the tremor. The veteran of two hundred sorties and seventeen victories was losing it, and he knew it.

He had seen it in others and the others didn't last long. "A pane of glass," he said to himself. "A fighter pilot's edge is like a pane of glass. Everything is so clear, so simple. You must only see what is in your sights. The other senses take care of the dangers. You feel the P-51 on your tail; you don't have to see him. You feel the chill on your spine; the hair on the nape of your neck stands up and yells, 'alarm, alarm, you are in grave danger.' "

He sipped again. Bruno was aware that he was talking out loud to himself. He could see the younger fellows at the next table staring. He didn't care. Instead, he continued, "The edge is so definite and so powerful and yet so fragile. Strain and time crack the pane, and eventually you no longer see. The alarms no longer sound."

That said, he drank the last little sip, smacked his lips, and ran his tongue over his front teeth to taste the last of the cognac. With more anger than tradition, he dashed the glass against the fire place. Maybe the B-17 was simply lucky that my guns jammed. Maybe their guns jammed too.

His own words provoked Bruno's imagination and his memory. He had heard of the temperature - humidity shift at altitude. If it fouled his guns, it surely could have fouled theirs. Closing his eyes, he tried to recall the gunnery pass. The low squadron was his choice, the aircraft on the extreme left of it. In his mind, the stick went over, left aileron roll, the bomber loomed larger in his sight and now upside down, check the arming switches "on", frame target in reflector sight, press trigger- nothing. Pull back on the stick, split-s. In five or six seconds the pass is over.

Bruno's eyes opened wide. No return fire, none at all. Theirs fouled too. He began to laugh, quietly at first, then heartily. "*Ha, ha, ha, ha.* The war took a holiday today. *Ha, ha, ha, ha.*"

At the next table, a young officer leaned back to see the cause of the levity, "Sir, what can be so funny?"

"The war took a fucking holiday. *Ha, ha, ha.* You wouldn't understand and either would the kommander, but I don't care." Bruno pulled his chair around so as to join his interrogator. "You see, when the war takes a holiday, nobody gets killed. Not even reckless fighter pilots. *Ha, ha, ha, ha.* Now give me a drink of your cognac, you misers." He motioned to the mess steward, "Bring a clean glass, please. I'm celebrating my last Christmas."

Ted Zackiewicz flew only one more mission before being sent home with frost bitten fingers. In his last mission, Teddy saved his fellow waist gunner from bleeding to death, but had to take off his gloves to do it. That day the "Darlin' Jean" wore new nose art which had a strong resemblance to Daisy Mae, complete with black shorts and a polka-dot blouse. The only departure was she still had red hair. Ted never shot down an enemy plane and he never forgot the one that got away. It had yellow cowling, a modeled gray paint job, and guns that jammed at just the right moment in history.

Bruno Hoelker led a gruppe of twelve fighters in an attack on Allied airbases in Operation Bodenplatte, ten days after the holiday cease fire. While attempting to land at a neighboring airfield, low on fuel and with a badly damaged plane, he was shot down by friendly anti-aircraft fire. He died in a military hospital the following day, 2 January, 1945. The epitaph on his grave stone reads, "Die Torheit des Krieges lockt viele Opfer an." ("The folly of war lures many victims.")

THREE

THE LONG WAY HOME

The second snowfall of the winter blanketed the ground when Freda Schroeck stepped from the front door of her home. She struggled with the clasp on her woolen cape; then pulled her scarf tight around her head. At first she walked slowly, but soon felt the winter bite on her legs. Her pace quickened. For a half minute she followed the road, then angled off through an open field toward the commissary.

Manfred had told her to steer clear of the camp perimeter and stick to the road. The morning was cold, and the short-cut would save five minutes each way. She would take the shorter way this one time.

Fresh snow crunched beneath her every step. She could see Manfred's boot prints made at day-break as he headed for the camp's manufacturing plant. He began every day early, organizing the labor force for another twelve hour shift. Jews, Poles, gypsies, Communists and resistance fighters from all over the Reich made up this force, and Manfred managed them with the same zeal and precision with which he battled the

Russians at Kursk, Smolensk, Minsk, Pinsk and all the others.

Her mind wandered back to the beginning. The Communists nearly gained control of the union in the Düsseldorf plant. Then National Socialism took over the government, and the Stutz-Staffle, the war and now the camp followed. It had all started with good intentions, stop Communism, put the people back to work, and make Germany strong again.

Freda asked herself, "How had it come to this, this wretched labor camp near the tiny farm village in Poland?" Manfred was a good man when he took the commission in the Waffen SS, intelligent, well educated, handsome, and his family was well respected in Dusseldorf. She was proud to be his wife and accepted his religious difference. The war was changing everyone and Manfred was no different.

He had fought bravely on the Russian front. His decorations included the Reider Kruz with Oak Leaves and Swords. "He was a national hero, why was he sent here to this hell-on-earth?" She knew the answer, but didn't dwell on it. Manfred's thesis for his advance degree was "Labor Management for Repetitive Manufacturing." The people in Berlin read it, promoted him to obersturmbann- fuhrer, and sent him to Poland. They claimed he had seen enough war; this was his reward. Manfred and Freda thought otherwise. Manfred would much rather have a battalion of Tiger tanks than a throng of slave laborers in a stinking factory where death was the only holiday. Only to her would he say it though.

Looking north into a clear blue sky, she watched the smoke columns belching from the stacks. Dark grey billows seemed to hug the horizon for miles eastward toward Russia. If the wind shifted, the fly-ash would settle all around the camp. The gray dust of a thousand victims would change the pretty mantle of snow to a ghastly reminder of the other part of the camp, the part Manfred forbade her to talk about.

She wondered, could all of this been prevented? Am I partly to blame? Or was I powerless in the face of such evil? And what of Manfred? He was drawn into it with good, honorable goals and now, who knows? Freda paused for a moment, trying to answer her own questions. Answers didn't come.

She continued on, feeling the chill of the wind, pulling the cape closer to her ribs, the ugly, ominous fence looming closer. She could see the large electrical insulators bulging from the wooden poles and beyond a group of fifty or so prisoners were forming into two lines. Along the fence line a ways, a tower guard leaned from his perch, then waved when he recognized her. She nodded politely.

Only fifty meters from the group of prisoners, Freda caught a tiny detail which stuck in her subconscious. For a brief moment, it did not surface to her consciousness. The short, stocky man with the wire-rimmed glasses was wearing a Roman collar.

"Oh, God, a priest," Freda cried. The tower guard turned, glancing down at her, shrugging, turning away with indifference. She covered her mouth in horror. "A priest, she said again. "We're killing priests."

Her knees grew weak She sank to the ground, hands quivering, shoulders shaking uncontrollably, her eyes filling with tears. They blurred the solitary figure with the round glasses and the white collar. Thoughts raced through Freda's mind in rapid succession.

The residue of her morning coffee mixed with her saliva, welled up behind her lower lip, then spilled onto the powdery white snow. With her face only a hand's width from the snow, her vision restored. The priest was clearly visible while those around him were still distorted and streaked with tears. Freda was still sobbing bitterly, when the priest turned, staring directly at her, he raised his right hand high above his head, blessing her with a sweeping sign of the cross. That might be expected, what followed was not. The priest, in the midst of hell-on-earth, smiled broadly, placed his hands together and bowed slightly. Freda heard him say in German, "I am your humble servant, God bless." Despite the distance between them, the words fell on her ears as a whisper.

After an indeterminable time, the sobbing ceased. When she looked up, the priest and the other prisoners were gone. The tower guard rocked on his feet and fanned his arms back and forth to keep warm. He appeared oblivious to Freda's presence, preferring to watch his breath condense like a puff from a cigarette.

Rising to her feet, she wiped the tears from her eyes and face. In minutes she was to the commissary where she completed her shopping. Slowly she walked home, her cape open at the neck, her scarf stuffed into her pocket, the cold no longer her concern. She took the long way home, the way Manfred preferred. It gave her time to pray, something she hadn't been doing.

FOUR

S.O. 137, OPERATION CYCLOPS

ay, 1943

M *For months the Japanese terrorized the American soldiers and marines on Guadalcanal with a psychological weapon. Almost nightly, a twin engine bomber, with its engines intentionally out of sync, visited them. Although the 50 Kg bombs did little damage, they did occasionally inflict casualties. The psychological effects were much greater. Deprived of sleep, the marines did not function as well the next day. Worse yet, they were frustrated that the aircraft that ruined their sleep, did so with impunity. The lack of night fighters in that theater of operations left them vulnerable to what had become known as the "Tokyo Express."*

Unknown to the marines in the foxholes or to the Japanese, a plan to put the "Tokyo Express" out of business was gaining momentum. Outside the ops tent sat a brand new F6F Hellcat. A camo net hid the plane from above and hid the silver bomb shaped protrusion which hung on its wing.

Inside the ops tent, Lt. Arlon Tucker (USMCR) read the latest radio message, "Special Operation 137 shall be implemented immediately. Authority to put the plan into practice as outlined to Headquarters Fleet Air Arm is hereby granted. Secondary target may be attacked at the discretion of the pilot. Good luck."

Finally, Arlon thought, we get to shoot back in this psychological warfare crap.

When radio operator, Cpl. Davis Hodge, saw that Arlon was through reading, "Do you know what all that means, Lieutenant?"

"Yes, I know exactly what it means. Now we'll see if Cyclops can do what I think it can."

"Cyclops, Sir?" asked Hodge.

"Yeah, that Hellcat out there with the silver bubble on its wing."

"Oh, you mean the radar."

"Yes, that wonderful gizmo that the Japs don't know about except what they read in *Popular Mechanics*. As soon as the ops officer comes in, I get briefed. Then we check the weather man. If conditions are right, maybe the Tokyo Express will get derailed very soon, and we can get some sleep around here."

Just then the tent flaps parted and the ops officer, Capt. Ed Hayes, entered, plopped himself down on a dilapidated folding chair. His map case hit the table with a puff of coral dust. As he fumbled for a cigarette, "It looks like Special Operation 137 is a *go.*"

Tucker glanced at Hodge, then back to Hayes, "Good news travels fast around here. I guess because there's so little of it."

With a flip of his Zippo, Ed Hayes ignited his Camel cigarette. After a long deep drag, he exhaled, filling the small tent with smoke. Arlon strolled to the flaps, tying them fully open. "Goddamn, Hayes, with one puff of that thing, you've managed to contaminate the entire area. Can't you save it for later?"

With the cigarette gripped between clenched teeth, Hayes

continued, "Relax, you may have a mission tonight." Smoke rose up to his eyes, forcing him to squint. "I've already seen the weatherman and it looks good. Clear with ten mile visibility, clouds ten to twenty percent at five to seven thousand, winds from the south-east at twenty, and no moon. Now here's the catch. We're depending on a low pressure depression to save us some fuel. As it passes from east to west, the winds should reverse for the return trip. I'll admit that's iffy. The front could stagnate and be in your face coming home. All things considered, it looks like a *go*, Cowboy."

Arlon flinched slightly at the mention of his disliked nickname, but didn't object. The low pressure thing whirred in the back of his mind, "Low pressure is counter clockwise in northern latitudes and the reverse in southern latitudes."

As Arlon brushed the coral dust from the chart, "We'd better get started. We've taken two of the guns out of the F6 and two guns only have two hundred rounds each. If I can't nail this bastard with five hundred rounds, he deserves to get away." Arlon looked at Hayes' drooping cigarette ash, and then continued, "The fuel situation is critical. We're on the ragged edge even with the weight loss of the guns and ammo and gain of two full belly tanks. I'll drop the tanks right after I switch back to the main. If the winds don't cooperate on my return, I'm gonna get wet."

Hayes placed the dividers on the map, stretched them open, then compared the distance to the scale of miles at the bottom of the map. "Sure as hell are," he said as he took his last puff and flicked the butt through the open flap. "The key to this whole operation is to shoot this asshole down in his own backyard. We want the Japs to know that we are no longer vulnerable at night, and we want them to know exactly what's happened to their aircraft. If we shoot him down here over our own positions, they won't know what's happened."

Across the tiny table, Arlon looked eye to eye with Hayes, "I understand that, Sir. Now what's this about a secondary target?"

Hayes pulled an eight by ten glossy from his map case, "The aerial photo shows a large building just off the north east corner of the runway at auxiliary field K-14. It's partially obscured by palm trees and the roof is painted camo. It may house the back up aircraft or fuel supply, probably not both. If T.E. works out of the main field at Rabaul, and not this one, you'll get wet for sure."

Hayes started to take another cigarette from the pack, but reconsidered. The longer they talked, the stuffiness in the ops tent became more so. As the sun rose higher, steam rose from the canvas sides. Perspiration beaded on foreheads, then formed little trickles on the men's faces. It was hot, like every other day.

"You've been picked for this mission, Tucker because you can squeeze the most out of an airplane, and this one is a stretch. It won't be like shooting down Yamamoto, but it will get their attention. It could make them act a lot more cautiously with their reconnaissance to say nothing about getting a night's sleep around here."

Hayes craved another cigarette, but resisted, then continued, "After you shoot down "T.E," radio 'The train is off the tracks'. You can tell us about any secondary targets when you return. Finally, if you have to go into the drink, radio 'Cyclops is thirsty,' and give your position. Your radio freq is written here." He pointed to a spot at the bottom of the aero chart.

Hayes could wait no longer. He fired up a Camel, his hands trembling. As he took his first drag, he sighed as though the great drought had ended. "We have a PBY scheduled to leave here thirty minutes before your ETA. His call name is 'Raspberry-two', his heading three-three-seven. Our call name is 'Mesquite'."

Arlon fanned the smoke with his map case, "Your call name is 'Mesquite'?"

"We thought it would make you feel at home," Hodge

added.

As Hayes rose from his chair, he shook Arlon's hand, "Good luck, Tucker. You'd better get some rest."

"I'll rest after the sun goes down and it cools down to ninety degrees. Right now, Ziggy and I have to tune that bird 'til it purrs. After that, we'll check the radar. I'll be ready for bed by then."

OOO

Pestered by the heat and more than a few mosquitoes, Arlon rested fitfully for about four hours. Slowly, he lifted his head from the pancake of a pillow. Faint at first, but growing in volume, *mmmuuummm, mmmuuummm, mmmuuummm,* the "Tokyo Express" approached.

Arlon jumped to his feet, sat on his cot and cleared bugs from both shoes in the prescribed manner. If any scorpions or spiders fell out, he didn't see them. Without lacing the worn out brogans, he raced to the protection of the trench.

Despite his quick response, two huddling figures had beaten him there. "Evenin', Lieutenant," a voice said from the dark. "Evenin', gents," Arlon replied. Just then, *wham, wham,* bombs exploded on the opposite side of the camp. *Wham, wham,* two more hit to the south. Cursing, swearing, and vulgarity reserved only for marines and Turkish jailers issued from the muddy trench. Tired, hot, angry men unleashed their frustration at the unseen enemy. When the engine noise had faded to a whisper, Arlon jumped from the trench.

With long, loping strides, he covered the two hundred yards to the F6. Ziggy stood by the aircraft holding his parachute. Quickly, Arlon strapped himself to it, climbed the rungs up the side and into the cockpit. In seconds, he was ready. "Clear," he shouted. "Clear," came the reply.

Two thousand horsepower worth of Pratt and Whitney whined, sputtered, and coughed a cloud of smoke. The rush of prop wash swept it to the rear and into the darkness. In his landing lights, Arlon could see the steel mesh taxiway rushing past. In a few seconds he was onto the runway. The F6 was not fully lined up with the runway when the throttle went to the full position. The engine roared, breaking the stillness of the tropical night once again. Fire, invisible in daylight, shot from the exhaust ports. As the square winged fighter rushed down the runway, its airspeed increased, until lifting gracefully, it took to flight. Cyclops-one was airborne. Special Operation 137 was indeed *a go.*

At eight thousand feet, Arlon leveled off, throttled back and trimmed the aircraft. After adjusting the prop pitch and mixture, he checked the gauges. He didn't have to. Arlon knew when the F6 was on the edge of the performance curve. He could hear it, feel it. I'm the brain of this robot, this robot that sees in the dark like a bat. With that, he threw a switch. The eerie muted light from the radar screen came to life, illuminating Arlon's face a ghoulish green.

Now where is that bastard? The radar swept left, then right. A bright blip showed at ten degrees. The sweep continued to work as Arlon watched intently. Heading three-three-six degrees, distance twenty miles. T.E, you are under surveillance, you prick.

For a few moments his attention was distracted from the scope as he checked the engine settings and trim. When Arlon looked back he had gained five miles on T.E. Damn, I'm running too fast. I'll fly up his butt. After throttling back still more, he adjusted the mixture ever so slightly, checked his air speed indicator. Minutes later, the distance was still fifteen miles, the engine still in the zone. T.E. was flying straight for home and the fireworks, Arlon thought.

Occasionally, he talked out loud to himself, reminding, reassuring. The check pad on his knee demanded the fuel checks each in their time. Arlon's pencil jotted the results. The instrument clock ticked. Another fuel check. Good man, Cyclops, you're right on schedule. Just west of Bouganville, the belly tanks dropped, fluttered aimlessly to the sea.

At eight thousand feet, he did not need oxygen. The mask never got latched, and the mic inside it waited for the one all important transmission back to Mesquite.

At five AM, Arlon noticed the glow of dawn in the sky to the east-north-east. To eliminate the possibility of T.E.'s gunners seeing him, he dropped his altitude to five thousand feet. After retrimming and setting engine settings, he closed to five miles. T.E. was losing altitude, obviously headed for the auxiliary field, not Rabaul.

OOO

Lt. Yoshi Tanaka smiled when he saw the makeshift landing lights illuminate the runway at Auxiliary Field K-14. To him the lights said "Welcome home," after a long trip. Tanaka throttled back, lowered his flaps to 'full.' As he reached for the gear handle, Tanaka heard what sounded like rocks hitting his aircraft. With his hand still on the gear handle, a .50 caliber bullet tore threw the aircraft's skin, two structural ribs and slammed into his wrist.

Before Tanaka could scream in pain, two more ripped through his chest and into the fire wall. Blood splattered the instrument panel as glass showered the floor. Tanaka's copilot froze in terror as he watched his commander slump forward, restrained only by his harness. As the port engine exploded, the darkened cockpit illuminated with a yellow flash. The copilot grabbed the controls, but to no avail. The normally graceful G4M dropped its left wing, skidded almost vertically and struck the ground. The resultant fire ball lighted up the south end of K-14, silhouetting the palm trees like a travel post card.

Shaken from his sleep by the gunfire and explosion, Maj. Ossi Akawa, K-14's base commander, rushed to the window. The funeral pyre of the G4M was at its apex. Across the runway, Akawa could see guns flashing as Cyclops-one raked the maintenance hangar at the opposite end of the field. Then the hangar exploded violently, sending one half of the corrugated metal roof folding on top of the other. Akawa strained to identify the aircraft, his feet barely touching the floor.

Behind him, the floor erupted in a hailstorm of splintering wood. Clay dishes and statuary disintegrated on the desk and table. Bullets tore through the thin framing members of the roof, exiting through the floors and walls. Akawa dove out the unglazed window, landing heavily on his shoulder. As he rose to his feet, the air raid sirens began to sound, slowly at first, then up to full volume and frequency. How ridiculous, the enemy is already gone. The perimeter guns never fired a shot.

In his bare feet and underwear, the major walked slowly to the radio shack. What might be my last transmission to headquarters, cannot wait until sunrise.

Arlon Tucker climbed to eight thousand feet, leveled off and retrimmed. He fussed some with the engine settings, then hit the mic button. With one hand holding the oxygen mask in front of his mouth, "Cyclops-one to Mesquite, come in."

A startled Davis Hodge tried to lift his head from the little table, clear his half sleeping mind, and wipe the drooling saliva from the side of his face. "This is Mesquite, go 'head, Cyclops-one."

"Cyclops-one to Mesquite, the train is off the tracks. Over and out."

"Mesquite to Cyclops-one, Roger that. Over and out."

Arlon tried to reposition his butt, as the pack he sat on was getting harder by the minute. Occasionally he cleared his tail with a couple of quick turns. Mostly he flew, checking gauges, listening for irregularities, feeling every vibration of his aircraft, the fuel gauge getting more attention than the rest.

The sun sat balanced on the horizon when Arlon saw Raspberry-two go by in the opposite direction. He wagged his wings, but did not break radio silence. "Twenty minutes to go and the needle's beginning to bounce on *E*," Arlon muttered. He knew he was nit-picking, but reset his throttle, mixture and prop pitch. "This thing could run out a hundred yards short for want of a cup full of gas."

With the field in sight, he began a gentle descent, trading every foot of altitude for ten feet of distance. With the throttle almost to 'idle,' He called Hodge once more, "Cyclops-one to Mesquite, come in."

"Mesquite to Cyclops-one, go 'head."

"Cyclops-one to Mesquite, clear the deck, I'm comin' straight in. Can't do this twice. Over."

"Cyclops-one, you are cleared for straight in."

Hodge, Hayes and a half dozen others stood by the ops tent and watched Cyclops-one land, taxi to his mat and shut down his engine. Arlon climbed slowly from the cockpit. He walked in circles in an attempt to reduce his butt fatigue, all the while unlashing his parachute.

"Helluva job, Tucker," Hayes extended his hand and shook Arlon's briskly. Ziggy the crew chief was next in line. After congratulations, he climbed up a ladder to Cyclops-one and put a dip stick into the main tank. Shouting to his pilot below, "You had lots of gas left, Lieutenant."

Arlon slung his chute from his back, "Oh yeah, how much?"

Raising the dip stick as if all could see, Ziggy replied, "Gallon, maybe a gallon and a half."

(*Laughter.*)

Ziggy did a double take as he noticed Arlon's shoes, "Oh, Lieutenant, your shoes are untied. You could trip and hurt yourself."

(*More laughter.*)

Hodge shook Arlon's hand. Holding out a piece of yellow carbon paper, "I thought you might want this for your scrap book, Sir."

"I don't have a scrap book, Hodge, but maybe I should start

one." With a wrinkled brow and blood shot eyes, Arlon read the intercepted and deciphered message.

FROM: COMMANDER K-14
TO: HQ FLEET OPERATIONS, RABAUL
DATE:*/ */ 1943

HAVING EXPERIENCED THE LOSS OF BOTH AIRCRAFT, WE HAVE SUSPENDED OPERATIONS AT K-14. ENEMY HAS AIRCRAFT WITH NIGHT VISION EQUIPMENT. AWAIT FURTHER ORDERS. CASUALTY LIST TO FOLLOW.
AKAWA, MAJOR

Except for the small group of squadron mates, nobody on Guadalcanal knew what Special Operation -137 had accomplished. Ten thousand soldiers and marines didn't cheer for Arlon Tucker. They didn't have a party the next night either. They slept. Arlon Tucker was not given any award or medal citation for "Special Operation 137," nor did he expect one.

Although the Japanese maintained their base at Rabaul until late in the war, K-14 was never again used. The Tokyo Express was derailed by one man. Armed with the new technology of radar, he had the ability to turn the enemy's terror machines and his fearless warriors into skeletons.

In 1947, Catholic missionaries returned to New Britain and occupied K-14. Priests and brothers patched the holes in the floors of the huts and removed the damaged roof on the hangar. After modifying the hangar into a gymnasium, they taught five foot Melanesians how to play basketball.

FIVE

THE MECHANIC, PVT. KAROVICH

March, 1945, near Zvolen, Czechoslovakia

Oberst Eric Hostedtler watched helplessly as the last of his FW-190 aircraft was put to the torch. Several black columns of smoke rose high into the sky, angling east towards Russia. Each aircraft roared with flame, then folded to the ground in a heap of unrecognizable junk. He'd fought the Communists since 1937, and now in this rugged area of Eastern Europe, defeat stared him squarely in the eyes.

Lt. Heinz Pritzer stood by, torn by the same anguish that gripped his commander. The colonel closed his eyes, sighed deeply, "This is what the end looks like, Pritzer. You should have been here when we were winning."

"I would give the rest of my life to have been here in '42 and shooting down a hundred Russkies. Seven missions is not a great contribution to the war effort. I never really felt like I'd become a fighter pilot." He could not look any longer and cast his eyes to the ground, "Ironic that my aircraft should be the last to be destroyed."

"We could have made a good fighter pilot of you, given a few more missions. It usually takes ten to fifteen. Lucky for me, the pilots I faced in Spain were as green as I was."

The words had left the colonel's lips but a few seconds when four artillery shells hit the base. One clipped the legs from the water tower, sending the contents splashing to the ground. Another hit the last Kubelwagon, tossing it upside down like a play toy.

Hostedtler flinched, but made no effort to take cover. The world could end at that moment in time and it would've suited him fine. Soon the hoard of brown clad Russians would swarm the airdrome looting everything of value. Slowly, he pulled a fine gold watch from his wrist, placed it atop a fence post. With the butt of a Walther P-38, he smashed it to pieces. A vision of his late wife passed through his mind. Monica wasted away her life waiting for me. I went off to war, and she stayed home only to die in an air raid. There is a lot of irony in wartime. Now she and her gift are gone forever. Only misery can follow.

Pritzer glanced briefly at his despondent commander. He wished he could have lightened his agony even a little, but words failed him.

OOO

The next day, Hostedtler sat in a chair in what had been his headquarters.

Rain dripped through the flimsy roof, soaking the wooden floor planks,

seeping through the cracks to the earth below. Opposite him sat a Russian air force captain leafing through stacks of papers.

"At last we are ready to begin, Colonel. For the record, state your name and rank," said the swarthy Russian.

Resentment surged through Hostedtler, This nomad from the Russian steps is going to interrogate me? He probably has never seen a toilet or had a glass of champagne.

"Colonel, your name and rank," the Russian repeated.

"Oh, yes. My name is Eric Hostedtler, Oberst, Luftwaffe, Luft Armie two."

"Good. Now we are getting somewhere. My name is Captain Propokov."

Before the interrogator could continue, Hostedtler interrupted, "Captain, I believe we can save each other a great deal of trouble. My Russian is better than your German. I can also converse in English, French or Spanish if any of those would be better."

Propokov's eyes enlarged, his lips pursed, then his face calmed. When he thought about it, speaking Russian was more fitting. After all, we are winning this war. Why should we speak some other language? "Very well, we will speak Russian," he quipped in his own tongue. His bushy eyebrows raised and fell as he spoke.

Hostedtler smiled as though he was satisfied, but inside he was saying, "You insufferable shit, you haven't even scraped the surface of the German language. You sound like a baboon trying to converse in orang-outang."

Again the papers shuffled for a minute, then the captain started once more, "Have you ever taken an oath to Adolf Hitler?"

After a pause, Hostedtler answered, "Never, only to Germany. This was required to become an officer."

'How many Russian aircraft did you destroy, Colonel?"

"In aerial combat, one hundred and twelve confirmed. I had another five unconfirmed and several on the ground. I did not keep count of those."

Rearranging his waist and shoulder belts, the captain tried to mask his annoyance at the arrogance of this claim. "Do you expect me to believe in such a huge number?"

"In front of you is my log book. I just saved you the trouble of adding them up. In the front of the log, you will notice that five I-16's were shot down in Spain. They could have had Russian pilots in them also, but then we have no way of knowing that. Do we?"

For a moment, only the sound of the dripping rain and the turning of pages filled the air. The captain nervously fingered the pages of the log, occasionally his face disfigured with surprise. "Six in one day, four of them IL-2's. Did you know that I flew IL-2's?"

"Perhaps, one day I shot you down, Captain," Hostedtler said with a grin. He would like to have said, "Flying an IL-2 is like driving a dump truck. You should wear a gold tire on your chest instead of those wings." The suggestion that he may have shot him down was caustic enough.

"I think not. I was only shot down twice and both times by ground fire," Propokov said as he closed the log book. "It appears that all of your unit records have been destroyed. Why not this?"

"The squadron and gruppe files were official documents which I was ordered to destroy. The log book is my personal record which I hoped to keep after the war."

Propokov moved a second pile of papers. Removed the first two sheets from the stack, "The Russian mechanic, Pvt. Karovich, what did he do?"

"Mostly he ate our food and drank our beer when we could get it. Mechanic? I thought he was a cook."

"That's all?" asked Propokov.

"Well, he did cook for us. Rather jovial fellow, always smiling. He played a concertina, one of those little accordion things." Hostedtler leaned forward, closer to Propokov, glanced to either side as if to be sure no one else could hear. "Between you and me, I think he was poisoning us."

Hostedtler was lying, but the captain appeared interested in the poisoning theory. "How did he do this poisoning?" He

38

asked.

"In the remote bases, we had a lot of dysentery. For all I know, Karovich was pissing in our stew, or worse."

Propokov leaned forward, "Did anyone die of this poisoning?" His eyes grew large again.

"Not that I know of. What he was doing was keeping us on the ground. The higher you go, the worse you feel. The higher you go, the more you have to go, when you have dysentery. If you get my meaning. Bacterial sabotage I call it. I could never prove it though."

Propokov wrote a page and a half during the poisoning theory discussion, but the truth was much different. It was Karovich who taught them how to start an engine in sub-zero weather. Karovich who devised the filter press to recycle engine oil when it became scarce, and Karovich who repaired batteries without a manual.

Skillfully, he took them apart, replaced bad cells, then magically resealed them with a hot poker. His day to day work kept the planes flying, but to divulge this to Propokov would send Vasili Karovich not to Siberia, but to an early grave.

With a fresh pencil in hand, Propokov continued, "How did Pvt. Karovich come to be in your unit?"

"He was captured with another man by Wehrmacht troops, and since they were air force, they were given to us to guard. The other man was killed by one of your artillery shells, three months ago. I believe his name was Shmansky or Shamansky. I'm not sure."

Propokov scribbled some notes on his pad. Blotting some water from the paper, he continued, "Did Pvt. Karovich ever receive monetary payment from you?"

"Me personally, or from the German government?"

"From the German government?" Propokov replied.

Hostedtler laughed lightly, faking his response. "No, Berlin could not keep track of us. I have not been paid in four months. Do you really think the paymaster would send money to a

Russian prisoner?"

"I suppose not, but we must ask these things. What about personally?"

"No, not personally." Hostedtler lied again. Shining boots, purchasing beer and vodka, other menial tasks, earned Karovich token rewards. The slightest bit of truth could be incriminating.

Early on Hostedtler had recognized that the questioning regarding Karovich was serious business, but now he wasn't sure whether it was he, Karovich or both of them who were in jeopardy. The Russian occupational law was being made up piece meal and there was no telling what this was leading to. The testimony, therefore, had to be believable, and at the same time separate Karovich from collaboration, himself from fraternizing.

Feigning indifference about the Russian mechanic appeared to be the best approach for Hostedtler, for his sake and Karovich's.

Propokov held his pencil with both hands, twirling it several times. "Did your men ever give money to Pvt. Karovich?"

"Not that I'm aware of. He was more trouble than worth, not exactly a gourmet cook who would be tipped generously by the men. By the Geneva Convention, we had to feed him, and by it, he could be made to work for it."

More papers shuffled, a new stack pushed to Propokov's front. "To continue, did you ever bomb or strafe civilian targets such as homes, hospitals or factories?"

Hostedtler gazed at the floor to his left, trying to weed out the implications of the last question. "Factories can build baby cribs or T-34 tanks. From the air we have no way of knowing which. We never intentionally strafed or bombed civilians or hospitals. Does that answer the question?"

Propokov scribbled more on his pad and turned to a new sheet. "I shall note your reply. You understand, there may be additional questioning later, by myself or others."

Visibly irritated by the notion that more questioning was forthcoming, Hostedtler spoke up, "I have nothing to hide, Captain. My men and I are soldiers fighting for our country. We did not ask to come to Russia or Czechoslovakia. We were sent here, just as you have been."

Without looking up from his writing, Propokov said, "You may go now, Colonel, back to your quarters."

The door swung open, as if by itself when Hostedtler approached it. Waiting outside for his bout with the interrogator, Lt. Pritzer stood nervously. A frown wrinkled his forehead, his teeth clenched.

If the young lieutenant was not warned, the cover story on Pvt. Karovich would certainly be ruined, and any pledge to Hitler would be disastrous. Hostedtler stared intently, hoping to get Pritzer's attention. As they passed, Hostedtler spoke, "Karovich only cooked, paid no money, you never vowed to Hitler."

Pritzer looked back at the colonel, the words sinking in as if orders on a combat mission. He repeated them to himself. Hostedtler could only hope that the gravity of the situation had registered.

Rain continued to fall, and Hostedtler pulled his poncho over himself, pushed his head through the opening. The Russians occupied the buildings, so his "quarters" were the hastily constructed compound of barbed wire. As his hands slipped to the bottom of the pockets, he felt his cigarette case. Somehow it had escaped the search of the marauding Russians.

Twenty meters away, in the next compound, he could see the mechanic, Pvt. Karovich. Hostedtler wasn't sure why he had gone to such lengths to protect him, perhaps spite for Captain Propokov, maybe a debt to Karovich for his help, or perhaps a shred of humanity planted in his heart by Monica. He would never be sure.

Lt. Heinz Pritzer spent ten years in a Russian prison for waging wars of aggression against the Soviet Union. He never killed an enemy soldier or airman.

In 1958 he joined the West German Air Force and was trained into F-84 jet aircraft.

Oberst Eric Hostedtler spent ten years in a Russian prison for waging wars of aggression against the Soviet Union. When he was released in 1955, he crossed the border into West Germany in a prison uniform. He carried with him only two items, his pilot's log book and his cigarette case, the other gift from Monica.

Pvt. Vasili Karovich spent six years in a Soviet gulag for surrendering to the enemy. When captured by the Wehrmacht, he was armed with a crescent wrench. In 1955 he immigrated to Romania and then to the United States. He became a citizen in 1961.

Six

JEEPERS, CREEPERS

L t. Bill Guthrie pressed the top of the brake pedals, and the shiny, silver P-51 Mustang lurched to a halt. A couple seconds later the huge four bladed propeller stopped and the Merlin engine went silent.

No ordinary mission had Bill just completed, not that any mission could be ordinary. In the four hours and thirty-two minutes since his takeoff roll began, he accomplished a feat that few other pilots did in World War II.

The stress of the ordeal had sapped the last bit of adrenaline form his body. His mind now a total blank, Bill sat in the cockpit, unable to move. His blue eyes transfixed on the instruments in front of him, he could not even feel the perspiration that soaked his shirt and ran down his spinal column.

Slowly, mechanically, he opened the canopy, unlatched the oxygen mask. The frigid air that swept into his cockpit should have been a stimulant, but it wasn't. With trembling knees, he tried to stand up. He could not. The knees that once carried him up and down the football field with the ease of a Greyhound, now shuddered, then gave out all together. Bill slumped back into the seat. The radio cord and oxygen hose were still plugged in, but he was unaware.

Out of the pea soup fog that had been his mind, came a song. It was Margaret Whiting singing "Jeepers Creepers." A wide smile covered his face for a few seconds, then disappeared with the song.

The music no sooner gone, when Bill realized that someone was at his side, leaning into the cockpit. "Take this, Bill," a voice said. The flight surgeon held out a two ounce glass of whiskey. It took several sips to get the first ounce down. The last one he threw back like a steel worker on a Friday night binge.

"Thanks, Doc. What was that stuff?" Bill asked. "Spiritus fermenti," Doc replied. "Oh, it tasted like whiskey." Doc smiled, knowing Bill's dry whit, then slid off the wing to check on the others.

In a few minutes, Bill would have to go to the ready room and debrief the G-2 officer. He struggled to remember the many events, but they seemed so fragmented, so garbled. One event overlapped another. He wasn't sure of anything except that he'd been in a hell of a fight.

The thumps of footsteps on the wing root told him his crew chief was there. Squinting against a setting sun, Bill looked up at him, "I think we got some today, Smitty."

Sgt. Ernie Smith let out with a rebel yell, clapped his hands repeatedly. He proceeded to do a three hundred sixty degree pirouette on the wing root. His feet tapping toes-down like a Flamenco dancer. "Goddamn, goddamn. I knowed it. I knowed it the minute I saw the gun ports all black." As he looked towards the crew chief on the next plane, Smitty hollered, "Hey, Lard, we got some today." Smitty still had his hands cupped together like a megaphone, when he realized he didn't know how many "some" was. Turning back to Bill, he leaned into the cockpit, looked closely at his pale complexion. "You all right, sir?"

"Yeah, just need a minute," Bill answered.

No longer able to restrain himself, Smitty asked, "How many, sir? How many did ya git?" Bill raised his gloved left hand, then opened his fingers, all of them. "Five, sir?" Smitty asked.

His eyes got larger by the second as he awaited a reply. Bill nodded three times.

"Oh my God. Five. Oh my God. Five all t'once"

Smitty could say no more. To him it was the World Series, the Cotton Bowl and the Heavy Weight Title rolled into one. He dropped from the wing with a thud, and disappeared behind the adjacent aircraft. Another rebel yell echoed above the tarmac.

Slowly the order of things was coming back to Bill's mind, but he still could not stand up. Twice he tried. Twice the legs trembled and gave out, but the brain was working again.

"Bandits at nine o'clock," the radio sang. Sixteen Me-109's were on a convergent course with the squadron. The CO was carefully positioning himself behind and slightly to the right of the enemy formation.

In a minute they were sliding closer to the enemy's rear. They must think we're one of their own, Bill thought to himself. Again the radio, "Red-two, take the one to the leader's right."

"Rog, Red-leader," Bill responded.

Bill had never, in his previous fifteen missions, held the enemy in his cross hairs. So close, he thought. He could see oil paths on the underside, soot near the exhaust ports. "Ready, aim, fire," came the radio call. Flashes of tracers filled the air ahead. Bill mashed his trigger. Immediately, the left wing tank of his target erupted in flames.

What followed was orchestrated chaos. Planes were breaking to pieces, smoke, flames, and radio chatter filled the air. Another Me-109 turned sharply in front of him exposing a huge projected area. Again Bill pressed the trigger- hits thudded all over the enemy's cockpit. "He's dead," Bill said into his mask.

Into a sharp right turn, Bill cleared his tail, making sure nobody was chasing him. Then back to the left, "Nobody there," he spoke again. He was supposed to be flying wing for his CO, but he was nowhere in sight. Sharply turning circles of fighter planes filled the sky. Each plane trying to out turn the other, get on his tail and shoot him to pieces.

With peripheral vision, Bill caught another Me-109 coming from the left at a forty-five degree angle. With a good lead ahead of him, Bill fired a long burst. The enemy plane flew into the shot train so that hits raked him from stem to stern. It went into a slow roll, exploding like samara from an elm tree, the wings detaching, floating and fluttering earthward.

For the next several minutes, Bill turned sharply, one way, then the other. All the time craning, stretching his neck to see behind him. Below, a dogfight was in progress. Two '109's on the tail of a single Mustang. They're not watching their asses, Bill thought as he put his plane into a diving turn. With the added speed of the dive, he overtook the turning '109's and closed to one hundred yards of the trailing craft. The first burst from his guns sawed off a four foot section of the right wing. The enemy craft snap rolled, pieces flying from the cowling, access panels leaving the engine compartment, a shower of debris narrowly missing Bill's Mustang. Then the disintegrating plane went into a rolling vertical dive and into a cloud.

The pilot of the leading '109 probably did not know that his wingman was gone. He didn't have much time to find out. Bill's gun sight filled with the image of the German plane, larger and larger. In the tight turn, Bill felt the g-forces pulling the blood from his head. Calmly, he rolled in ten percent up-flaps, and watched as the cross hairs passed through the enemy plane. His guns pounded, tracers flying, the fifth victim trailing a long, oily, cloud of smoke, until it went vertically into the ground.

Less than a hundred yards from a stone farm house, it burned a circle of black on the earth. As Bill pulled out of his dive, he saw livestock in the same field, grazing as if nothing had happened.

No more details surfaced from his subconscious to the conscious, except that he was filled with anxiety on the return flight. Protecting his CO was his prime responsibility and for the first time in sixteen missions, he had lost him.

Finally, Bill pulled himself to his feet, disconnected his oxygen hose and radio cord. Nearly thirty minutes after landing, the CO put down, taxied to his hardstand. Bill breathed a sigh of relief, heading for the skipper's aircraft, anticipating the dreaded chewing out. He didn't get a chance to apologize. The skipper vaulted from his Mustang, embraced Bill in a bear hug. Grinning from ear to ear, "Ya gottem, Billy Boy, ya gottem both. Yahoo!"

"Got both what," Bill asked.

"Why the two Heinies on my tail, who did ya think? The CO continued, "I'll confirm the other two that you got while we were still in formation. Four Gerries in one mission. That's unbelievable."

"Five, Colonel, the lieutenant got five, sir." Smitty said as he crawled from beneath a Mustang.

"Did anyone confirm the fifth?" the colonel asked.

Bill's face wrinkled with concern, "Well no, not yet anyway."

Smitty looked at the colonel, then back at Bill, "Maybe the gun camera saw it. We'll know tomorrow."

"Amazing," sighed the CO, "in one mission, my wingman nails more Krauts than I have in thirty missions. I can't wait to see the gun camera films."

As Lt. Bill Guthrie lay in bed that night, his mind raced and sleep didn't come easy. Most of the boys would give anything to do what he had done that day, but his feelings were mixed. He wondered about the five German pilots he shot down. "Are any of them alive tonight? Probably not," he concluded. And too, he wondered if he would shoot down others before the war ended. Would some hotshot German ace shoot him down?"

The thought of professional jealousy crept into his mind, the seeds of it resounded in the colonel's words, "My wingman, etcetera, etcetera." He'll probably transfer me to another squadron. But then again, I did save his butt, even if I didn't know it was he. That wasn't the first time either. Maybe he will keep me around. I'm a wingman, not a shooter. The events of the day squeezed the truth out of his thought. Well, maybe I don't shoot half bad.

By morning, Smitty had painted four black and white crosses on the fuselage and a bold set of letters on the nose, "Jeepers Creepers." After the camera film was developed, he painted the fifth cross. Strangely, the only time the camera worked was to show the deflection shot that nobody else could confirm.

With all the new trappings, Bill's shiny P-51 was no longer anonymous. Neither was Bill Guthrie, he was an ace. He could sing, *"Jeepers, creepers, where'd ya get those peepers? Jeepers, creepers, where'd ya get those eyes,"* all he wanted.

SEVEN

SINK THE NISSHIN

July 22nd, 1943, the Solomon Islands

The replacement pilots for Marine Torpedo Squadron VMTB-143 had not yet recovered from the long voyage from the States. Coral dust, mosquitoes, and unrelenting heat added to their misery. It rained so often that some puddles around the airfield never dried out, mosquito larvae wriggling freely.

H. Clark "Casey" Stalnaker, a slender Georgian, hid from the sun beneath the canvas of a two man tent. His fair skin already sunburned, he didn't want it any worse. White zinc ointment colored his nose like a circus clown. "God, it's hot," he blurted.

Jim McQuade, a fellow pilot from Whitewater, Wisconsin, chuckled, "On the Russian front Germans are freezing to death, seems like we could spread the heat around some." Just then the alert horn blared from the ops tent. "Something's up," Casey mumbled. In two minutes they were at the tiny ops tent. It overflowed with pilots trying to gain the advantage of shade. Casey grinned at the foot wide riverlet that coursed though the tent like some form of field latrine. Muddy brown water looked suspicious.

The ops officer counted heads, making sure all were present. With a pointer jabbing at the large framed map, he began, "It's here off the Island of Bouganville; the Japs have a rescue convoy coming. The prime target, and your only target, is an 11,000 ton seaplane tender named the Nisshin. It is escorted by two destroyers and two cruisers. Ignore the escorts until the tender is sunk, and then you're free to go after them."

"What's so important about this seaplane tender?" asked a voice from the crowd.

"Fifteen hundred infantrymen," replied the ops officer.

Casey stroked a three day beard, "A battalion of replacements is headed for Guadalcanal?"

"Actually, they're headed for their garrison at Buin on Bouganville, Stalnaker. Each aircraft will carry a single 1,000 pounder. Our orders are 'To drop on her until she sinks.' This will be a long mission, maybe five hours. Scattered high cumulus from 12,000 to 18,000 feet with fifty to sixty percent coverage, wind from the south-east at ten. Takeoff is in thirty minutes, gents. Okay Bulldogs, go sink the damn thing."

OOO

Wind blew though the open canopy of Casey's TBF torpedo bomber. It was cooling, refreshing, but still humid. His flight suit was still damp and clammy, but a whole lot cooler at 12,000 feet. A sixty percent cloud cover might hide the enemy's ships, he thought. Well, we'll cross that bridge…

Sixteen other TBF's formed around the squadron leader Royce Coln in addition to Casey's. An eighteen ship formation assembled and sixteen Dauntless dive bombers soon joined above and to their right. "Impressive, eh what?" he said into the crew intercom as the formations flew past a towering cumulus buildup. The noonday sun bleached it white as it stretched and boiled to the clear blue above.

Two and a half hours passed slowly. Monotonous flying except when they dodged the monster cumuli. The engine purred. Radio silence finally broke when Coln excitedly called out, "Bulldog-one to Gearshift, target spotted, 6 degrees – 33 minutes south, 156 degrees -10 minutes east. We are attacking." The time was 13:53.

"Bulldog-one to Bulldog squadron, attack by divisions."

OOO

Aboard the Nisshin, Captain Ito Jotaro barked the order for a hard turn to port. Waves washed over the deck on the starboard sweeping gunners from their positions. The "emergency" horn whooped. Thirty-four fighter bombers raced at his ship from two separate attack angles. It appeared that Ito's tactic had worked as bombs exploded off the starboard beam. He was doing an incredible 34 knots.

Ito's luck soon ran out when a huge explosion rocked the Nisshin's No. 2 turret on the port side. Heavy black smoke poured from the gaping hole. Orange flames leapt skyward through the billowing smoke. Frantically, he called for a damage report. Before he got his reply, he ordered the forward magazines flooded to prevent the fire from spreading. His speed reduced to 15 knots. The ships bow, weighted with the flooding, plunged deep into every wave. At 13:56 two more bombs struck as the attacking Avengers followed the dive bombers.

OOO

Diving from 12,000 ft to 3000 ft, time goes by quickly. Anti-aircraft tracers flooded the sky from every direction as the Bulldog squadron raced to the attack. Airspeed indicators bounced on 300knots. Flack bursts buffeted every plane in the formation. The bomb released with a clunk from Casey's P-81 aircraft, *The Loose Goose*.

Stalnaker pulled up out of his dive at 1500 ft. Over his shoulder, he barely caught a glimpse of his bomb burst amidships, but the tail gunner saw it fully. Screaming with excitement, Frank Henning watched as the Nisshin rolled and plunged bow first into the rolling sea. In a minute it was gone. The huge fires snuffed in an instant and only a pall of black smoke hung low over the sea. White foam swirled, but not even an oil slick marked her burial. Escort vessels continued their relentless barrage. Flack bursts and tracers in great profusion followed, and yet they could not find a single TBF even as they withdrew.

As the squadron reformed, Tom Morris radioed that his engine was acting up. Two others throttled back to fly escort with him. Morris was tweeking every setting to get the max performance from his laboring engine. Better than two hours from home and nothing but ocean patrolled by Japanese ships lay in front of him. He waved at the two other pilots, and then the "thumbs up." The remainder of the squadron disappeared within twenty minutes, leaving the three behind. Morris looked at his two mates, smiled nervously. A radio message without a call sign broke the sound of the wind and the sputtering engine, "Thanks guys."

OOO

Thirty minutes passed after the main body of the squadron landed, and no radio call came to ops headquarters. Concern for the three aircraft and their crews mounted. Finally, the ops radio crackled, "Bulldog three to Gearshift, over."

The operator answered, "Gearshift to Bulldog three, go ahead."

"Bulldog three to Gearshift, we are in sight of the field. I'm coming straight in, escorts will follow, over."

The men on the tarmac cheered as Tom Morris applied his brakes and shut down the engine. As mechanics removed the cowling, a crowd gathered in front of his TBF. From the fourth step of his ladder, a mechanic shook his head in disbelief, a large 40 mm unexploded shell protruded from the bottom cylinder. Thousands of rounds were fired at VMTB-143, but only one found its target, and it a dud.

The fortunes of war are strange. Within minutes the Nisshin was attacked and sunk. Not a single Marine aviator was killed, but 539 of the 630 soldiers aboard the Nisshin were lost. Of the ships complement, 546 were lost making the total 1,085. Marine casualties: one man wounded, gunner Caryle W. Vorachek. The remaining Japanese reinforcements had been dispersed among the escort vessels and were returned to Rabaul.

Unknown to the Marine aviators, they had also destroyed 22 tanks and 8 artillery pieces, plus food, ammunition and medical supplies carried by the Nisshin. The impact of the losses canceled any chance of a Japanese counter attack on Guadalcanal. Admiral Hulsey telegrammed VMTB-143, "Well done.."

OOO

One Year Later, Santa Barbara, CA
A band played Sousa marches. A small contingent of friends and relatives looked on with pride as the Distinguished Flying Crosses were presented to thirteen Marine pilots: Royce Coln, George Smith, Everett Horgan, Norman Glenn, Earl McLaughlin, Tom Morris, Jim McQuade, Casey Stalnaker, Charles Loiselle, Jim Yeast, Morgan Webb and Ed Leidecker. A Purple Heart dangled from Cpl. Caryle Vorachek's chest. Col. Perry O. Parmelee presented the awards after a brief speech.

With no losses to the Marines, the unbelievable mission was a disaster to the Japanese. Captain Ito Jotaro was promoted posthumously. Later events would not be so kind to the members of VMTB-143. Within weeks of the ceremony, Jim McQuade flew into a fog bank and was never seen again, Casey Stalnaker was killed in a flying accident in 1948. George Smith and Jim Turner were both killed in action in the Korean War. Their squadron mate Jim Painter never left the Solomons. Tragically he was shot down, and taken prisoner by the Japanese. The Navy Dept believed he was being taken back to the Japanese mainland, when the ship was sunk by one of our own submarines.

The others lived long enough to see their children grow up, and some their grandchildren. No man can outrun or out fly his destiny.

EIGHT

THE BUTTERFLY BOMB

October 1940, England

The war had not come to Lowestoft in Suffolk, as it had to London and Coventry. The little town by the North Sea had seen German bombers passing overhead, but bombs never fell. So no alarms sounded when the lone German plane flew over at a low altitude, its engines roaring.

Seven year old Tommy Singleton, just home from school, could see the black crosses on the wings. He even made out the form of a man sitting in the nose. "It's a 'einkle, Mum, a 'einkle," he shouted.

Tommy's mother leaned out the upper window to tell Tommy to get back inside the house. As she looked up to glimpse the vanishing plane, something caromed off the roof across the narrow street, and smashed into the leaded glass transom over her front door.

As glass tinkled to the floor inside and to the stoop outside, Tommy saw the device hanging from the torn beads of lead. He'd never seen anything like it. Bright orange it was, with yellow spots, like a gaily colored butterfly.

"Don't touch it," Mrs. Singleton screamed from the window. "Ah can't, Mum, it's up too high," Tommy replied.

OOO

Lt. George Ogeltree examined the gadget that hung from the shattered transom. With clipboard in hand he tried to sketch it before deciding on a plan of action. In his first week on the job with the U.X.B. detachment, he'd already defused two one hundred kilogram bombs and now this thing that wasn't in the manuals.

With minimal training he had been successful with the others, but this "thing" with the garish paint job, was totally foreign, totally frightening. Worst of all, it was impaled on the jagged arms of lead beading. Miraculously, the blue glass fleur-de-lis center piece was still intact. George marveled at the blueness of the glass and the blue light that passed through it to the floor below.

No group of experts surrounded the young lieutenant as he completed his rendering. He was totally on his own. His only allies were to be his wits and an engineering degree conferred just four months earlier. What were they thinking of, I'm a civil engineer, not mechanical. I shouldn't even be here, he thought as he placed a step ladder in front of the stoop. With camera in hand, he ascended. Now just three feet from this booby trap for children, he snapped away. Each time he changed positions while advancing the film with a click.

Leaving the ladder in place, he studied the monster intently, ten inches across the wings, and three inches deep at the center. George added the dimensions to his sketch.

His mind wandered, as George put the sketch pad and the camera at safe distance with his tool box. He could not imagine anyone in the whole of England devising such a bomb, a bomb which clearly targeted children. He'd seen the Mark III time

56

delay fuse intended to explode after everyone left the shelters or headed for work. The Mark IV followed which had a tricky left handed thread causing the plunger to push into the detonator as you removed the fuse. That was diabolical, intended to kill U.X.B. men like he. But this was different, beyond the level of Jack the Ripper. "Der kinder bomb," he muttered. Those responsible, he was sure, would burn in hell.

Once more, George approached the bomb. The planning stage was over, and he knew he had to get on with it. The sun light was fading, and soon he would be working in the dark.

He felt sure that the detonator was operated by the wings. If one or both of them folded, *boom*, that terrible word that was never spoken by the U.X.B. people. *Boom*, the onomatopoeic expression that meant someone got blown to bits, was stricken from his vocabulary, but still in his mind. His first consideration must then be to secure the wings in the open position. From the second step of the ladder, George threaded fishing line through a small hole in the left wing. After tying a knot, he ran the line to the right wing and did the same. "Considerate of Gerri to put the holes there," he thought as he pulled the string tight.

"So far, so good," he said out loud, "part-A is complete. Now for Part-B."

Part-B was to secure the bomb vertically before he cut it loose from the lead beading.

Using Tommy's fishing pole, George pulled out a length of line. Looking up, searching for something to loop the line over, but nothing seemed to serve the purpose. The answer lie in his tool box, a little eye bolt with a screw thread on the other end. This he threaded into the frame of the transom above the glass. With the fish line through the eye bolt and tied to Part-A, he had skillfully completed Part-B. The fishing pole held tight by closing the adjacent window on the handle. With the drag on the reel firmly set, George began Part-C.

Perspiration soaked his shirt as his side cutters snipped

away at six small lead beads. Before he knew it, the bomb was free and dangling from the fish pole like a herring. Carefully, George opened the window and withdrew the pole. Stepping up the ladder he snipped the eye bolt with the side cutters. Part-D was to walk the whole contraption to the outskirts of town, place the bomb on the opposite side of a thick stone wall and detonate it with a pre-positioned charge. It sounded easy, but with every step, the bomb bounced a little at the end of the pole.

Despite the connection string, the wings moved. George slowed his pace. He would have given a month's pay to not have his uniform blouse on at that time, but it was too late to be removing clothing. "The catch of the day could remove everything," he said, again speaking to only himself.

As the last streams of light faded in the western sky, Lt. Ogeltree pushed the plunger. The charge and its partner bomb flashed and boomed, the report resounding across the landscape. Ogeltree fell to one knee, puking his lunch out, retching with each attack of nausea, his shoulders lurching violently. The town's people rushing to his aid and comfort, stopped to allow him to regain his composure. They rushed again to his side, when again he stood erect. Tears welled in his eyes. He was breathing slowly, deliberately, as the accolades poured from his admirers, "Ya did real good, lad," "What's your name, son," and lastly, "I brought ya a pint, Luftenant."

George took the pint and never stopped tipping until only the foam remained. The bitters washed away the taste of puke and the fear and everything that was evil. "I'm Luftenant George Ogeltree, reluctantly at your service", he exclaimed with a laugh. "I'm afraid I'm not very good at this sort of thing."

The people laughed with him and walked him back to town and the pub. Tommy Singleton scurried by his side, carrying his fishing pole, chattering incessantly. In the pub, everyone who would look and listen got the story from the excitable seven year old.

As the bitters continued to flow, and the crowd sang "For He's a Jolly Good Fellow," George removed his tie and uniform blouse. He joined in as they sang "It's a Long Way to Tipperary", "There Will Always Be an England," and several others. Closing time at the pub was delayed a full hour that night. For a few hours, the war was far away, and reality drowned in the foam of the bitters.

At the War Crimes Trial at Nuremberg, in 1946, Major George Ogeltree pressed for prosecution of those responsible for the butterfly bombs, but his pleas fell on deaf ears. The prosecutors had bigger "fish" to fry.

In his book, "Their Finest Hour," Winston Churchill described the U.X.B. detachments thusly: "Somehow or other, their faces seemed different from other men, however brave and faithful. They were gaunt, they were haggard, and their faces had a bluish look, with bright gleaming eyes and exceptional compression of the lips; withal a perfect demeanor. In writing about our hard times, we are apt to overuse the word 'grim.' It should have been reserved for the U.X.B. disposal squads."

After sixty years, old Tom Singleton still shows people the hole in the transom, the piece of cardboard that keeps out the winter gales, and his fishing pole. A photograph of a young lieutenant adorns the mantle above the fireplace, and Tom will tell the story of Lt. George Ogeltree and the butterfly bomb to anyone who will listen. In that long and painful war, there was only one war hero in Lowestoft, Suffolk.

NINE

A CHRYSANTHEMUM FROM JOSEPH

Japan, April, 1945
An airdrome on Honshu

The last survivors of fighter Squadron 210 rose from their seats, cheering, throwing their caps to the ceiling. In the fervor of the moment, all twelve had just volunteered for a suicide mission against the American Fleet off Okinawa.

Nobody noticed, but Lt. Joseph Noguchi had hesitated for a split second before standing. In the smallest of time frames, Joseph had come to a decision he knew he would have to face for over a month. The decision was a difficult one for several reasons. The first being, that Joseph was a Catholic. In a nation mostly Buddhist, Joseph's ancestors had accepted the faith from Jesuit missions nearly three centuries earlier.

Schooled in his religion from the age of six, he would have gladly died a martyr's death for it. Now he was faced with the near certainty of being a martyr for his country and his emperor, but not his faith. As the general delivered his impassioned speech, Joseph considered the suicide issue. The Church did not, and never would, condone suicide. But in his mind, Joseph was not willfully taking his own life. Death would come as a result of his attempts to destroy his country's enemy. His cause was the delivery of a bomb on a target. The cause and effect issue had surfaced in theology courses. That was classroom; this was real, real life and real death.

The general droned on. Joseph day dreamed as he wrestled with the issue. First, he imagined himself falling on a Samurai sword, then a pistol to the temple. Somehow crashing a nearly new Shiden 11a didn't seem like suicide in the true sense of Hari-Kari.

As Joseph played theological tennis with his conscience, another player entered the game. He had weathered the prejudice in college and again in the air force. Even his first name was the mark of a Christian. It could have been Hideyo, like the famous bacteriologist, or Isamu, like the sculptor, but it wasn't. It was Joseph- the name given him at his Christening. He would never change it. To do so would deny his patron saint and his religion in one act of deception.

Twice passed over for promotion, the young warrior let the disappointment melt, then evaporate. He would end the war, or the war would end him, a lieutenant. If the latter, heaven awaited him, not deification as the Bushido tradition claimed. Joseph would live with Christianity, and if need be, die with it. The prejudice issue had tugged in the opposite direction, but not strongly enough.

The deciding factor had seeped into his mind and into his heart, his family. When the moment of truth arrived, he must stand up and cheer, or remain seated and silent. He pictured the general and the other eleven pilots staring, glaring at him. Worse than their scorn, what would his family have to endure? Prejudice in a country with only one race and one language can be just as cruel as anywhere else in the world with multi faceted cultures and languages. His father, a noted marine biologist and personal friend of the emperor, would be shunned from the scientific community. His younger siblings would be denied any opportunity for advanced education.

In the split second after the general ended his speech with a fever pitch, Joseph Noguchi, knew what he must do. He stood with the rest; he cheered with the rest. Feigning the exuberance of his compatriots, he had just signed his own death warrant.

An airdrome on Kyushu

Dawn broke with streams of orange light breaking through the high cumulus. "It's an omen, Joseph, today we will become immortal," Capt. Akahito shouted as he pointed to the sunrise. The first group of four aircraft was already taxing by to the runway. Their engines roared; the prop wash stirred the straw colored grass beside the pavement. No cheering spectators lined the runways. That was for propaganda films.

Joseph tied the white silk scarf around his head, the red circle emblem of Japan centered on his forehead. Two other lieutenants, Atachi and Heshakawa did the same. They drank no saki and visited no religious shrine. They simply bowed to each other, then to Joseph and then all three bowed to Akahito.

A minute later, all four mounted their aircraft and began start up procedures. They, the second four, were off. No crowds cheered them on either. The landing gear raised; the flaps came up. They climbed to fifteen thousand feet, five thousand above the first group and five thousand below the last.

Joseph tried not to think of his family, or home or old friends. It was too late for that. "I must concentrate on this mission," he thought, but many things ran in and out of his mind. His memory was dumping everything, like photographs from an old shoe box. He recalled the commander who railed him for not shooting at the hospital tents, "You Christians are too soft, your emperor demands more from you." Then his failings as a son and brother, marched by in orderly precision. The three hundred miles passed swiftly.

He could not bring himself to tell his family what he was up to, nor why. Instead, he wired his family's florist, and asked him to deliver one chrysanthemum They would have to understand that he was torn between duty, honor, religion and family. He could not satisfy all four.

His left hand found the crucifix on the chain around his neck. "Jesus Christ, forgive me all my sins and for what I am about to do. Life is so varied and confusing and my troubles are magnified by wartime. My western religion has collided with my eastern culture."

Joseph did not get a chance to add "Amen." The two Corsairs dove from out of the sun, guns blazing. Akahito exploded. Atachi's engine and wing tank burst into flames, and he spiraled down trailing black smoke. Heshakawa broke left, Joseph to the right.

A bank of clouds at twelve thousand feet was the only hiding place and Joseph dove to its sanctuary. As he looked over his shoulder to clear his tail, he saw Heshagawa's aircraft trailing smoke and diving at a forty-five degrees angle.

Both Corsairs were giving chase. In a minute he was into the clouds, staring intently at his instruments. Holding his original heading and new altitude for several minutes, he broke out of the clouds directly over the American Fleet.

He selected the carrier directly ahead to be his target. It loomed large even at ten thousand feet. Joseph rolled over into a half roll, pulled back on the stick. Tracers rose in long lines from a dozen locations. Black flack burst ahead, to the left, to the right, buffeting the Shiden.

Through a hundred, a thousand shells, he dove untouched, untouched save one. A forty millimeter shell passed through the propeller and exploded in the engine block. A bright light flashed for an instant, and then------ *Eternity.*

Mrs. Noguchi anxiously opened the tiny envelope, and read the card. It read only, "Joseph." The flower was beautiful. Not a cut flower, but potted in a clay pot with moss, a living thing.

Ten

Words That Rhyme

October, 1945

The young marine emerged from the taxi donning his garrison cap. After pealing three bucks from a money clip, he paid the cabby; then turned to face the Oceanside Cafe. The autumn sun was setting with a magnificent display. Reddish orange colored the sky, the ocean, and the white stucco buildings.

His class-A green uniform was perfectly tailored; the shoes spit shined to a mirror finish. On his arm, the stripes said he was a sergeant; the two rows of ribbons on his chest said he'd seen more than a little action.

But this marine was different from most of those who passed through this little town just west of Camp Pendleton. Taut brown skin and slightly slanted eyes were those of an American Indian. Sgt. Roy Crafton, USMC, scanned the neighborhood, admired the new manicured park across the street.

He pushed his way through the doors, the juke box playing a tune he'd never heard, the smell of fish frying, the smell of beer permeating everything.

Roy approached the bar, avoiding a waitress with a fully loaded tray, avoiding a spilled beer on the floor, arriving at the last bar stool just before it was taken. It had been three years, but he was sure this was the place. "Whaaat'll ya have?" asked the bartender.

"A draft beer, please."

As beer filled the frosted mug, Roy studied the bar tender closely. "Yep, that's him," he thought. The black hair parted in the middle was a clue, the drawn out "Whaat'll ya have," was the clincher. Although the handle bar mustache was new, it just made him appear more like a bit actor from a western movie.

"On the house, marine," said the bar tender as he slid the beer in front of Roy. "Much obliged," he responded. Roy smiled, and then turned to seek out a table, conceding the stool to another patron. Long ago he'd learned to avoid the bar, too many arguments, and too many fights.

Finding a table proved difficult. The famous Friday night fish fry attracted a good crowd, and who likes to eat at the bar.

As Roy slowly strolled toward the rear of the cafe, he took the first long sip of his draft. A thousand, no two thousand times, he had thought of this happening and he was savoring the beer and the moment. A second long sip was as rewarding as the first. "The islands could be so hot and beer can be so cold," he thought.

"Have a seat, marine," a voice from the corner barked. Jim Callaghan's leg gave the chair opposite a good shove and it bounced gently against Roy's shoe.

"Don't mind if I do. Is it always this crowded here?" Roy asked as he straightened the chair.

"Not really," Jim said as he folded his steno pad and parked the pencil behind his right ear. "Half of these folks will leave after the fish fry. My name's Jim Callaghan, what's yours?"

"Roy Crafton. I'm pleased to meet you." Roy looked at a sixty year old man with white, white hair and a red, red face. His tropical suit was clean but crumpled. Brown and white spectator shoes protruded from beneath the table. Jim Callaghan's hand shook Roy's, but Jim never left his seat. The novelty of the shoes tickled Roy. "They didn't wear those on the reservation or in the Corps," he thought to himself.

While Roy arranged his chair and placed his cap to one side, Jim noticed the rows of ribbons. He knew some. The Silver Star, the Bronze Star and the Purple Heart were all there, but he wouldn't have recognized the Navy Cross if it had been. "Looks like you've been around some according to the ribbons."

"Oh, yeah. The ribbons: the Canal, Iwo, Okinawa. I've visited some bad parts of the Pacific."

Jim's interest was peaked. He'd driven up from San Diego to get the scoop on the changing real estate market in Oceanside. The young kid seated opposite him sounded like more of a story than what filled the front of his steno pad. "Wow, Guadalcanal, Iwo Jima, I tried a few times to get interviews from service men, but they would never open up enough to make a story."

"What kind of a story?" Roy asked.

"I write for the San Diego Press. I'm a reporter. Done my own column for twenty years now." Smelling a story, Jim reopened his pad, checked the point on his pencil.

"What do you want to know? I'm a Navajo Indian. I think people should know that we've fought in the war. A lot of my fellow tribesmen are buried on those stinking islands out there."

Jim's eyes grew larger. He raised his hand with index finger high, "Sam, Sam, bring my friend a beer. Make it two." The bar tender nodded his approval. When the beer arrived, Jim was already scribbling his modified short hand.

"Okay. First off, why did you volunteer for the Marine Corps?"

Roy placed his glass on a coaster. Condensation ran down the frosted glass and into the cork particles. "I learned when I was a small boy that people don't give you respect. You have to earn it. I saw how my father was treated in business deals in town. They didn't assault him or anything like that. It was more of a low grade contempt. Shunned him as a person, and sometimes took advantage."

"Once, the broker we dealt with overpaid Pop by several hundred dollars. I don't think this man was always fair with my father. The quantities the broker had ordered were reduced, but his book keeper paid the original sum. The broker then went on a trip, and was out of town for a couple weeks. When he returned, Pop was at the train station with a check. After that, the broker was different. I think Pop had his respect."

"My father is a good man, and he helps other people a lot. He employs nearly thirty people and has others that do piece work. We use to joke about his favorite quip, 'Some day you have to answer to God if you cheat somebody. Don't matter if it's a million dollars or an ear of corn. God don't forget.' I guess that's good advice. 'God don't forget'."

"When the war started, I thought if I served in the Corps, I could tell myself that nobody is better than I, and nobody is more important. I think it was Edgar Guest who wrote, '*I can never hide myself from me; I see what others may never see; I know what others may never know, I never can fool myself, and so, whatever happens, I want to be self-respecting and conscience free.*' Does that answer the question? Maybe I got off the track."

"No, I think that was a good answer," as Jim turned a page. Somewhat surprised by the poetry, he continued, "Do you think you've gained respect?

"Yes, I do. The main reason I'm here tonight, in this bar, is because I was refused service here three years ago."

"In this place? Are you sure?" Jim asked.

"No doubt about it. I recognized your friend, Sam. He was the one. Tonight, he gave me one on the house. Also, nobody offered me a seat the way you did tonight."

"Maybe things have changed in three years," Jim muttered.

He continued scribbling, "How old were you when you volunteered?"

"Older than most, I was twenty-one, in the middle of my third year of school."

Jim flipped a page, "During your training or boot camp, did you feel that you were discriminated against for being an Indian?"

"At first, the drill instructors didn't know what they were dealing with; they just knew we were different. They leaned on us a little heavy. Once they saw we could take it, we got treated like every one else."

Jim knew the answer to his next question, but for the record he asked anyway, "Did you experience any discrimination in the fighting unit, your platoon or company?"

Roy thought a minute, rubbed his chin, "There were always jokes about Indians and fire water, Indians and cars up on blocks, stuff like that. We usually responded with Custer jokes. They say there are no atheists in fox holes. There are no bigots either."

Jim liked the response. His pencil scribbled on as his questioning continued. "Did the Corps give you adequate equipment for the task?"

"Once we were issued the M-1 rifle, it was. The First War Springfields were too slow. The other old weapons like the water cooled .30 caliber and the B.A.R. were good for the duration. Our leather shoes rotted and fell apart in the jungles. They need to develop something better for jungle warfare."

Jim was on a roll and the answers flowed freely from Roy. "What about the leadership, did you have confidence in your officers?"

"Our battalion commander on Guadalcanal typified the leadership. Major Puller is now a brigadier. Some day he will be Commandant of the Marine Corps. The platoon leaders and company commanders always performed to the highest standards. A lot of them died trying to get their jobs done."

Looking up from his pad, Jim said, "I'm going to ask some personal questions. At any time you can say 'I can't answer that,' and if remembering any of this becomes too emotionally taxing, just say so, and I'll continue on another tack."

Roy nodded. Callaghan continued with a series of questions mostly about how the terror of battle had affected him since war's end. Between notes, he stopped to look up and into Roy's eyes. From years of interviewing, Jim could read a person through their eyes, their mannerisms, and the waver in their voice. He was a human lie-detector machine, but he sensed nothing but honesty from the man across the table.

Jim lit a Camel, flipped the lid closed on his Zippo, "What was the scariest moment of your life, the time when fear was the greatest?"

"A Navajo is taught to treat fear as an outsider, not something that dwells within. Sometimes fear breaks down the barriers and gets to the mind and even to one's spirit. Such a thing happened on Guadalcanal, in October of '42."

"I was a one man listening post, two hundred yards in front of our battalion headquarters. We dug a hole big enough to sit in. They covered it with shrubs of some kind. It's one thing to fight with marines all around you, and quite another to fight surrounded by Japs."

Roy hesitated, wondered for a minute if he was going too far. Fortified with another swig of beer, he continued. "Sitting in the hole, alone and waiting in the dark was terrifying. About an hour after dark, it began raining. Sounds were coming from everywhere, but I couldn't tell what they were. The first recognizable sound was a shoe breaking suction of the mud. Then whispering followed. Only fifteen feet away, two guys were setting up a machine gun and tripod. I peeked through the shrub, my eyes barely above ground. Other Japs were sneaking past me. I could see the legs wrapped in those bandage things that they wear."

"I slid back down in the hole, as low as I could get. Then I put the telephone receiver up to my mouth and blew into the receiver four times. We had a code in case the enemy was too close to talk. One blast of air if it was a recon squad or sappers, two if it was a platoon, three for a company and four if it was, well four if it was 'big'. After ten seconds, I blew four times again. I was about to do it a third time when all hell broke loose. Mortars were hitting all around me - friendly fire isn't so friendly when it's falling on number one."

When Jim looked up from his pad, Roy's eyes were closed. In his mind he was remembering, reliving something most people would prefer to forget. "Jap officers were shouting orders, muffled cries from the wounded echoed through the jungles. Bullets zinged everywhere. Some even struck the shrub above my head. The rain got heavier. Then the machine gun next to me opened up. I was fifteen or twenty feet away and feeling totally useless. By then the rain water had poured into the hole and I was waist deep in it- cold. The two Japs were busy reloading when I snapped. I couldn't take it any more. I stood up in the hole and pitched a grenade over to them. One of them must have seen the grenade, he yelled "Yaaa." Then it exploded killing them both. I sat back down into the hole just before the explosion. I was determined not to get up again, but a few minutes later, I felt this tugging on my telephone line. I peered over the edge to see a wounded Jap holding the line. He was face down, muttering Japanese, and holding my phone line over his head. The rain must have unburied it, and he was trying to draw the attention of his comrades. I left the hole and killed him with my bayonet."

"After that, I don't remember much, except being really cold, and really scared. The attack only lasted about twenty minutes, but I stayed put until morning, when a squad of marines came out and got me. They put me on a stretcher because I couldn't walk. I was trembling all over, maybe in shock. It was eighty or ninety degrees, and they were wrapping me in blankets."

With eyes wide open, Roy added, "There is one other thing."

He paused as if ashamed to continue, "I was crying. Me, a Navajo, a marine, and I was crying. The stress was overwhelming. The battalion commander put his hand on my shoulder. He said, 'Son, what you did last night probably saved this battalion form being overrun.' I think he was being honest. The first mortar barrage caught 'em pretty good."

With tears welling, and then running down his cheeks, Roy rubbed his eyes as if to stem the flow. Jim squashed the cigarette into an ash tray, "We don't have to do this, ya know."

"No. No. It's all right. Please, go on."

Armed with a new pencil and a new cigarette, Jim continued. "What was the most difficult thing you had to do in the war?"

Roy drained the last of his second beer, "It's hard to say. Killing that wounded Jap was difficult, but it was probably burying friends. On Iwo they built a temporary cemetery when the fighting was over. After the bugler played "Taps" a verse of a poem came out of the back of my head. I recited it aloud, unrehearsed. I don't even remember who wrote it. *'Rest on, embalmed and sainted dead, dear is the blood you gave- No impious footstep here shall tread, the herbage of your grave. Nor shall your glory be forgot, while Fame her record keeps, or honor points the hallowed spot where valor proudly sleeps."* The strange thing is, when I should have cried, I didn't. Everyone held back. Didn't show their pain.," Roy added.

Jim had second thoughts about his next question, even hesitated a moment. Then asked anyway, "Did you ever feel that you had let your buddies down?"

Roy closed his eyes once more. He kept them closed while he answered. "Of course, every time one got hit, I blamed myself. I think everyone has the same reaction. If you don't blame yourself, you'll blame them, and that's worse. One time a friend got hit by a mortar. His arm and foot were detached, covered with blood and I was yelling at him to get up. He was dead and I'm telling him to stand up. Crazy. Just couldn't deal with it."

Jim looked at the ribbons on Roy's chest, "I see you have a Purple Heart ribbon. When did you get wounded?"

"A few days after that night attack on the Canal, I was hit by mortar fragments, both legs, shoulder, back, a regular pin cushion. A man nearby wasn't hit, but the concussion killed him. They said that his lungs collapsed. I always thought that very strange."

"Then what happened? Did they ship you back to the States?"

"Yes, after a stop in the hospital at Pearl, and then to the hospital at San Diego for rehab. When I was recuperating, it seemed to take forever. I used to start each day with what was more of a prayer than a poem. It was written by Ophelia Browning. Do you care to hear it?"

"Sure. Let me have it."

"*Unanswered yet? Tho' when you first presented this one petition at the Father's throne, it seemed you could not wait the time for asking, so anxious was your heart to have it done; if years have passed since then, do not despair, for God will answer you sometime, somewhere.*"

"When He answered, I went to Camp Elliott near here and trained Navajo code talkers. Then we went to Iwo Jima. Sometimes you have to be careful what you pray for."

Jim smiled broadly, "I know what you mean. What are code talkers?"

"Navajos who speak the native language over telephone and radio so the enemy can't break our code. All that is still classified, so don't write about it."

Jim nodded intently, "Makes sense. I'd never heard of doing that. Next question, where do you go from here? What are your post war plans?"

Roy lifted the third glass and took a swig, "That's the nice part. I'll go home and the elders will put me through the rite of purification."

"Rite of purification? What's that?"

Drawing an analogy proved difficult for Roy. Finally he said, "In the war, I was surrounded by good and evil spirits. The elders will persuade the evil ones to leave me alone and honor the good ones for sustaining me. Then they'll wash the blood from my hands, ritually speaking that is."

Jim leaned back in his chair, "I think I understand, like an exorcism, followed by the litany of the saints and a dip in the baptismal font."

Both men laughed at the analogy. "That's about it," Roy exclaimed.

A period of silence followed, before Roy added, "I'd like to go back to college. The Navajo people need leadership in government, business, and education. We can no longer depend on farming and herding sheep for an economy. We have too many sons and daughters."

As Jim assembled his sheets and added foot notes, Roy continued. "My immediate plans are to go home and reacquaint myself with the land of my ancestors. This is a beautiful time of year there. Reminds me of another poem, not a sad one like the other one.

Roy sat straight in his chair, rested the remnants of his beer on the table. Once again with eyes closed he drifted into his poetry. *'A haze on the far horizon, the infinite tender sky, the ripe, rich tint of the cornfields, and the wild geese sailing high; and all over upland and lowland the charm of the goldenrod - some of us call it Autumn, and others call it God.'*

Jim could no longer conceal his amazement, "Do you always recite poetry like that?"

"I had good teachers. They taught me how to mobilize my memory and to appreciate the written word. My Navajo friends have a nickname for me. Loosely translated it means 'words that rhyme'."

As the two men rose from the table, Jim said, "Before you leave. Talk Navajo to me."

The edge of Roy's mouth curled slightly into a smirk. He then ran off ten or twelve seconds of Navajo. "Okay, what does it mean?" Jim asked.

Roy's smirk broadened, "It is good that the white man listens to the tale of the Navajo. Custer did not listen to the tale of the Sioux."

The two were still laughing as they approached the front door. Jim stopped, held Roy's sleeve, "Hold on a second, Roy. I want you to meet Sam."

Hearing his name, Sam paused, awaited the introduction, then shook hands with Roy. After they had exchanged greetings, Jim continued, "Roy, here, says that you refused him service here three years ago."

Sam exhaled as his head drooped slightly, "Well, I guess that was a possibility. I don't remember that happening, but we had the 'blue laws' then. I couldn't serve any Indian, my apologies, Sergeant. This town, this country, has done a lot of soul searching since the war. We had Nissi American families, from right here in Oceanside, living in detention camps while their sons fought the war in Europe. Just wasn't fair."

Roy extended his hand again, "There's no need to apologize. The beer 'on the house' told me things had changed. I think Jim Callaghan's curiosity got the better of him."

OOO

Jim Callaghan's column earned several journalism awards for his story about Roy Crafton. Later articles about the Navajo Code Talkers earned still others. Jim's story about the changing real estate market got trashed.

ELEVEN

REMAINS: READY

7 MAR 1945

HIS MAJESTY'S WAR DEPARTMENT REGRETS TO INFORM
YOU THAT YOUR SON, FLYING OFFICER WOODROW K
DUNBAR, WAS KILLED 7 MAR, 1945 DURING A
CLASSIFIED MILITARY EXERCISE IN THE NORTHERN
COUNTIES STOP

FURTHER DETAILS OF YOUR SON'S DEATH WILL BE
RELAYED TO YOU AS THEY BECOME AVAILABLE STOP

REMAINS: READY

10 March, 1945

A single bell tolled its monotone again and again. Six pall bearers, dressed in RAF uniforms, slowly carried Woody Dunbar's flag draped coffin through the double doors and down the center aisle. In the front row of this small Gothic church near Ipswitch, Suffolk, his parents sat, well dressed stoics.

Half a dozen rows back from the front, two young women dabbed beneath their black veils to stem the flow of tears. Evelyn Hatch hadn't known Woody for very long, four months or so, but they were very much in love. Her friend, Lydia Craven, could have passed for her sister. In face and stature, they were alike in many ways, and today, dressed totally in black, the likenesses were even more evident. Only the shades of their lipstick set them apart.

At the altar, stood the aging vicar, wearing his black cassock and white surplice. His quivering voice unmasked his private grief, a grief specially reserved for one of his former altar boys.

A few other mourners completed the sparse attendance. Considering the family's social standing and the untimely death of a young service man, the church should have been overflowing. It wasn't. This was wartime.

Aside from the small congregation, the funeral setting appeared to be complete. It wasn't. Woody Dunbar's Union Jack flag draped his coffin, but Woody's body wasn't in it. Three bags of sand stood in for the young pilot, and the telegram which now sat folded in his father's vest pocket, contained yet another lie.

The training mission Woody had flown wasn't classified at all. The "secret" classification kept the family and the press from asking embarrassing questions. There were lots of those.

5 March, 1945, at an American bomber base near Leeds

The bottom hatch of the B-24 swung open and Lt. Perry Sessoms dropped to the tarmac with a thud. His parachute, leather helmet and oxygen mask usually came with him, but today they remained behind in the cockpit. Today was different.

Perry's usual calm demeanor was gone. Anyone who could read auras would have seen the red around Perry; for those who couldn't, the bulging veins on his neck were a give away. He was griped. He didn't run towards the ops building, but every step was quick and purposeful.

Over the door, the sign read, "British Air Attaché," and Perry didn't bother to knock before thrusting the door open. A startled NCO jumped up from his desk, "Can I help you, Lieutenant?"

"You bet you can. I want to see Squadron Officer Berkley, and it can't wait."

The NCO scurried to the interior door, knocked, then entered. In a moment, he was back, "The squadron officer will see you, Lieutenant."

Perry blustered into the small office. Squadron officer, my foot, this old fart hasn't flown a plane since 1918, he thought to himself. Berkley didn't look up before Perry began his tirade, "Squadron Officer Berkley, one of your Spitfires made a head-on gunnery pass at me this afternoon, and if he doesn't quit it, we're gonna blast him."

Berkley still did not lift his eyes, "My dear boy, when you report to me in a military manner, I shall listen to your complaint. Not until."

Perry snapped to attention, his face another shade redder. "Lieutenant Perry Sessoms requests permission to speak to the squadron officer," his arm cocked in salute.

Finally, Berkley looked up, slowly returned Perry's salute. "Now what's this about a head on pass from a Spitfire?"

"Yes, sir, that's what I said. One of your Spits made a head on gunnery pass at me. My top turret gunner asked if he could shoot. I told him no. Sir, we've seen JU-88's and ME-410's in our training area. We can't take a chance that it's a Spitfire using us for practice. The closing rate is nearly six hundred miles an hour."

Berkley stroked his gray mustache, "What do you expect me to do about it?"

Still at attention, Perry continued, "Sir, I expect you to

contact that squadron, and tell them to knock it off before someone gets hurt."

Again, Berkley stroked his mustache, "Very well, I'll pass the word along."

Perry Sessoms took a deep breath, then slowly exhaled, "Thank you, sir."

He saluted and did a snappy about-face. As he left the office, he heard Berkley mutter, "Probably couldn't hit him anyway."

Perry hesitated. He wanted to say, "We'll blow the SOB up if he does," but he didn't. Filing an incident report appeared to be more productive.

7 March, 1945

Perry Sessoms' crew had just delivered their practice bombs. The formation box hadn't been very tight, so the results were not expected to be great. Even the weather was not cooperating - scattered clouds with fifty percent coverage, eight to twelve thousand feet, winds gusting to forty knots from the north-west. The navigator on board was green as a string bean and they were a hundred-fifty miles from the home field. Perry was wondering what else could go wrong when the right inboard engine coughed three times. The tachometer bounced crazily between zero and two thousand rpm.

Throttling back to "idle cut-off", Perry feathered the prop to reduce drag, and then scanned the gauges looking for signs of a fire. "No fire, thank God," he said into the loose flapping oxygen mask. He made a left ninety degree turn and headed for home at ten thousand feet. Perry was feeling he had things in control when the intercom squawked, "Top gun to captain- Bogie at twelve o'clock, straight on."

Perry could see the tiny dot growing; the decision had already been made back in Berkley's office, "Shoot him, top gun." The twin fifties began pounding one long burst. Empty shells rattled against the metal floor behind Perry. So intent with trying to identify the bogie, Perry did not see it fly helplessly into the stream of lead. What he did see was a yellow-orange explosion that buckled the wings of the other plane and sent the whole flaming wreck wheeling past, barely sixty feet above him.

Sinking into his chair, Perry whispered into his microphone set, "Oh God, oh God, oh God, no." The vision of the buckling wings with the concentric red, white and blue circles was indelibly printed on his memory. "That wasn't a German."

Many men were killed because of military blunders in World War II. In July of 1942, convoy PQ17 lost twenty-three out of thirty-five ships when the Admiralty withdrew its destroyer screen. Faulty intelligence suggested a German pocket battleship was positioned to destroy the escort. It was not. U-boats and aircraft flying from Norway had a field day.

In April of 1944, as American forces trained in England for the D-day invasion, British destroyers were withdrawn without warning from Exercise Tiger. Two LST's full of men, equipment and gasoline fell before the torpedo attack of German e-boats. Bodies of six hundred twenty eight men washed ashore at Slapton Sands as so much flotsam and jetsam. Four months later, the distraught exercise-commander took his own life, six hundred twenty nine.

Woody Dunbar died because Squadron Officer Hillary Berkley shirked his duty. The irony of Dunbar's death was that he had never buzzed an American bomber before. Egged on by his squadron mates who had, he came to a violent, fiery death. The six pall bearers carried more than the coffin weighted with sand. For the rest of their lives, the weight of the guilt would be theirs to share with Hillary Berkley.

In quiet moments, for the rest of his life, Perry Sessoms would wonder, "Who was that guy in the Spitfire, and why did he die so needlessly?"

TWELVE

THE ENEMY ANONYMOUS

October, 1944
France, near the Belgian border

S gt. Don Veator hugged the ground. Pine mulch and red brown earth squeezed between his fingers. The bullet, which almost ended his life, drilled through the radio set exiting with a puff of wood splinters. The forest reverberated with the report like some ancient drum relay.

For a second, he and Pfc. Dave McMillan lie motionless. Both knew the sniper was close. The rifle's bang had burst from the forest only fifty yards from the source.

Four months in combat had taught them to think and react quickly. When they heard the muffled sound of a rifle bolt opening and closing, both went scrambling for the cover of the woods. Their M-1 rifles in hand, Don went right, Dave to the left.

After ten yards or so, Don slid feet first, like a runner going into second base. Slowly, he raised himself to a sitting position and nestled his back to a tree. The burst of adrenalin had him panting. Abundantly aware of the sound, he tried vainly to muffle his own breath with a muddy hand.

Immediately in front of him lay a ten yard patch of ferns. These gave way to a stand of pines eight to ten inches in diameter. With an eerie silence, the forest reacted to the rifle shot. Smell of the autumn pine sap filled the air with a heavenly aroma. The damp ground soaked his pants, chilling his buttocks, making him squirm, distracting his attention from the unseen sniper.

With his eye level barely above the ferns, Don surveyed the woods. He could have been back near Syracuse hunting squirrels. The scene was that similar, but the sport was much different. Someone out there was trying to kill him, and that someone had blown his first chance.

Forced into a game of 'watch and wait,' he could only hope that McMillan recognized the situation and didn't try anything foolish. With a quick glance, Don noted the time on his watch. It was three-thirty-five.

"In less than two hours, it would be dark. Then what?" Don wondered. "I have to be prepared to sit this out. Fritz may be thinking the same thing." He tried to get comfortable despite the wet seat and the first twinges of stagnant muscles. It could be a long wait, and evidently McMillan knew enough to stay put, he thought as he continued to scan the woods. His eyes strained, searching for any movement, any irregularity in color or shape.

As the earth continued to dampen his trousers, Don considered changing positions. Quickly, the thought was dismissed. Scanning left, then right, and back again, nothing appeared but the trees, the small shrubs, and the low growth of ferns. A gentle breeze swept through the forest, evergreens swayed.

The subtle sounds of the woods were returning. Birds pecked at insects in the bark. Acorns and pine cones tumbled from their lofty perches. In the distance, a G.I. laughed, and then called someone a "Dumb ass." Funny how sound travels sometimes, even in the woods, Don thought to himself. He wasn't listening for nature's sounds though. The snap of a twig, metal on metal, clothing scraping on a branch, anything like that would do, but he heard nothing of the sort. It was as if the sniper took his one shot, then evaporated with the puff from the rifle.

Several times Don wanted to check the time again, see how much closer to dark it was. He didn't dare. One look away could be fatal, so he continued his vigil. Fritz was out there somewhere, waiting for his second chance.

Don stretched his shoulders and back muscles, but only to the limits of good thinking. This could be a long wait, he thought as he continued to scan the woods. McMillan's safety was a concern, but the thought of him quickly vanished.

Everything looked the same as when he first began looking. Even the individual trees began to take on familiarities: the one with the big canker, the one with the light green moss, the one with the dangling, broken limb, the one with the huge, black blob of resin.

Again and again, Don's vision swept the woods. Again he saw the same trees and shrubs. Muscles and tendons resisted cramping, but the lack of movement was beginning to tell on them. Then, at the base of the tree with the moss, something new. A black jack boot protruded from behind the ten inch pine. A chill ran from Don's neck to the base of his spine. Was it there all the time? Had he been missing it? Or was it simply that Fritz couldn't stand still any longer?

Don raised his sights to approximate head height. I'll never know, he thought.

A deep breath followed by a half exhale and his trigger finger tightened. A black tipped, armor-piercing bullet plowed through the tree, through the steel helmet, then stopped on the opposite inside of the helmet. Fritz dropped in a heap. His right boot, still clearly visible, shook in a death spasm. To the left of the tree, Don could see Fritz's upper body resting face down.

His helmet still strapped in place.

The possibility of a second sniper lurked in the back of Don's mind, so he remained still for several minutes. The waiting got the better of McMillan, however. "Did ya get him, Sarge?" he bellowed.

Don Veator stood over the lifeless form of the man who had almost killed him. He didn't want to see his face or know his name. He didn't take his identity disk or the camo painted helmet with the hole in it. He did take the '98 Mauser with the large Zeiss telescope, and the bandolier of ammunition.

"Yeah, I got him," he finally answered McMillan. Don Veator experienced no joy, and he let out no cheer or battle cry. When at last he glanced at his watch, it was four-fifty-five.

Rays of the setting sun streamed through the forest illuminating the newly formed mist. Like a masterworks painting, the scene printed into his memory for good, the contrast of nature's beauty and the ugliness of man's war.

OOO

In one of the many ironies of the war, the '98 Mauser became the anti-sniper weapon of the 299th Engineer Battalion. When Dave McMillan test fired it at thirty yards, he shot a 1" pattern all in the "X." At two hundred yards, it was 3". As he handed the rifle back to Don, he said, "God must have a plan for you."

For many years after the war, Don enjoyed fishing for bass and pike, but not hunting and shooting. Although his boyhood hunting experiences probably contributed to his survival, his interest in hunting ended in a forest near Lille. Don Veator regretted naming the sniper Fritz. It made his enemy too personal, instead of more anonymous. Together he and McMillan buried the enemy sniper at the roadside, and then nailed his identity disk to a post. He never read the name on it.

THIRTEEN

THE LEGACY OF WARTHOG-ONE

...Having seized the initiative by our initial landing, we must insure that we keep it. The best way to interfere with the enemy concentrations and countermeasures will be to push forward fairly powerful armored force thrusts on the afternoon of D-day... I am prepared to accept almost any risk in orderto carry out these tactics. I would risk even the total loss of the armored brigade groups- which in any event is not really possible.

Montgomery to Bradley and Dempsey,
14 April, 1944

6 June, 1944, 13:00 hours

Still wet from wading ashore, the men of infantry Company-D stood in disbelief. An instructor sergeant pointed out the features of the Sherman tank like a salesman on a used car lot.

Thirty minutes earlier, they had been an infantry company preparing to move inland from Omaha Beach. Now they were getting a crash course in armored warfare.

Five days earlier, Lt. Chuck Franzen had been a platoon leader. Now, through a series of misfortunes, he was the C.O. of this company. He didn't feel prepared to lead twenty seven men, no less four times that many. A year out of college, a ninety day wonder, he'd never been in combat before, and yet he was expected to command and gain the respect of a hundred men.

The instructor mentioned almost in passing that the other crews had been "used up," whatever that meant. Company-D was expected to fill the void, not with three months training at Ft. Knox, but with three hours there at Omaha.

Although the assault on the beach was over, the rumble of artillery to the south distracted the students. Franzen glanced to his left to see their weapons lying there like so much discarded junk. M-1 rifles, Thompson's and B.A.R.'s, previously treated with meticulous care, now wallowed in the sand. An ominous feeling began to twist his guts. "This whole thing stinks," he thought to himself.

As the new drivers learned their trade, one Sherman after another arrived and parked close by, seventeen in all. Eighty-five men were selected quickly to man them. The rest gathered their weapons, and marched away in double file. Only the last man looked back, shaking his head, blowing the sand from his rifle, delighting in the fact he was not chosen. Sixteen men and one officer left to become replacements for another unit. Nobody seemed to know which one, nor where it was located. The word SNAFU entered more minds than one.

The new crews drove their tanks, then fired three cannon rounds into a cliff. With each round, the tank shook, the gun breech recoiled violently. Quickly, the training was over. It was 15:45 hours when a colonel arrived and shook Franzen's hand and wished him well. When Franzen asked, "Sir, what is my mission?" The colonel replied, "Why, son, take these tanks up that road and engage the enemy." His unlit cigar flipped to the other side of his mouth. The jeep left, skidding in the sand as it sped away, disappearing over a dune, it and the colonel never to be seen again.

A half mile from the beach, Franzen did a radio check with the lead tank. "Warthog-one to Warthog-two. Did you hear that crap about closing to three hundred yards of an enemy tank? Over."

"Roger, Warthog-one. I heard that," replied Lt. Len Kravitz. "They get to shoot at us from a thousand yards though. Isn't that against the Geneva Convention?" Even in the stress of uncertain battle, Kravitz had a sense of humor and for an instant Franzen smirked.

The column rumbled southward, dust rising from the road in a tell tale cloud. He was concerned about the dust and with good reason. They were approaching a gentle rise and soon they would be exposed to a full mile of open ground.

Franzen's mind was racing, so much to consider. The next ridge was a mile away and it would take nearly three minutes to reach it if they came under fire. Teller mines were probably sewn on either side of the road. "Would they encounter tanks or guns first?" he asked himself. The rumblings from the south suggested guns. As he pressed the radio button, "Load white phosphorous, set optical sight for one thousand yards," Franzen gave his first battle order.

With head and shoulders above the hatch, Franzen watched his number two take a hit on his left track. Just as Kravitz cleared the hatch, a second round exploded his fuel. Orange flame topped with black smoke shot from the tank straight up twenty feet in the air. Kravitz leaped to the ground, rolling as he hit.

When the second tank stopped, Franzen keyed his mic, "Don't stop. Go! Go! Go!" A shell struck the second tank knocking the turret askew. In rapid succession, the next two suffered similar fates. Explosions erupted all along the column. Metal plates flew in every direction, whirring as they did.

With cracking voice, Franzen screamed at his own driver, "Don't stop. Go! Go! Go!" Warthog-one, traveling on the left shoulder, passed the four disabled tanks; skidded wildly as it tried to regain the road.

"Road is zeroed-in, don't stop," he shouted into the mic. Behind him only chaos as all but Warthog-four, Sgt. Manly, took hits from the German guns. Manly weaved left and right, twice side swiping burning tanks, narrowly missing dismounted tankers, continuing on at full throttle. "Warthog-four to Warthog-one, I'm right behind you, Lieutenant."

Franzen glanced backward just as Warthog-four burst through the veiling battle smoke. Manly, disregarding the threat of teller mines, caught up to his leader just short of the second rise. A shell exploded aft of Warthog-one. Two more bracketed Warthog-four. Franzen looked to his left, the terrain tailed away beyond the rise, before him the enemy guns at last exposed. Their crews appeared to be re-aiming to a direction ninety degrees to their right. "Slow down, slow down, stop here," he ordered his driver. The two Shermans skidded to a halt

"Warthog-four, targets at ten o'clock. Do you see them?"

A quick response came back, "Roger, Warthog-one. Three artillery positions and six mortar pits."

With raised binoculars, Franzen surveyed the positions, "Warthog-four, take the gun in the center. I'll get the nearest one; next we both attack the farthest one."

"Roger, one," came Manly's reply.

Franzen's panic melted into a calm, dedicated determination. "Target gun, ten o'clock, range one thousand yards."

Pfc. Roger Kahn took aim. The turret motor whined above the idling engine. "Target up," he said firmly.

"Fire." The first shot fired by Company-D rocked the thirty-two ton tank. As Franzen watched for effect, Warthog-four fired his first shot.

The white phosphorous shell exploded, spraying white plumes, tossing bodies from the gun position, rendering it useless. With field glasses still in position, he watched the second gun explode. Its barrel cocked downward at thirty degrees. "Not bad for rookies," Franzen quipped.

"Load white phosphorous, target gun, nine-thirty o'clock, range one thousand yards."

Kahn responded again, "Target up."

Cordite smoke choked his voice as Franzen cried, "Fire." Again the shell incinerated the gun position. Warthog-four's second shot flew into the cloud of phosphorous smoke, accelerating its distribution with a thump.

Concerned that the white smoke would obscure the mortar pits, he ordered the next shot, "Load hi-explosive." The gun breech clanked shut.

"Warthog-four, start on the mortar pits. You start farthest and I'll start nearest."

"Roger, one."

One by one the mortar pits erupted in explosions. Warthog-one fired eight times, Warthog-four seven. Strangely, the mortar men never directed their fire at the two assailants. It was as if they and they alone out of the seventeen, were invisible.

"Cease fire," Franzen said into the radio mic, and then repeated it to his crew. Kahn continued to gaze at the results through his optical sight, "We sure put some hurt on 'em." Franzen didn't respond, but rubbed his eyes and forehead. The tanker helmet fell from his head, dangling by the radio cord. Looking back to the north, he saw the smoke rising from Company-D's tanks. "Driver, turn this thing around and head back." Pfc. Allen Gross locked the left track, spinning the tank, sending turf flying from both tracks. Slowly, he headed back towards the rest of the company. Warthog-four followed twenty yards distant. It was 16:15 hours.

Warthog-one rolled past the scattered debris that had been

Company-D. Medics treated the wounded, plasma bottles dangling from rifles, white bandages winding around heads and limbs, blankets covering the dead. Men with metal detectors scouted the shoulders of the road and beyond. Smoke and heat still gushed from some of the tanks. At the end of the destruction, men were placing bodies side by side. The blankets and tarps covered all but their boots. The row of boots seemed to go on and on, like a vanishing point drawing in Art-101.

The tank stopped short of the row of dead men. Franzen slipped down the side and over the track. With his black hair tossed wildly and his face torn with anguish, Franzen stared without blinking. He dropped to one knee. The shock that strained his mind and body would not let him cry. The empty stomach would not let him vomit, he could only retch. Saliva dripped from his lower lip.

A friendly voice penetrated the numbness, "Are you all right, Chuck?" It was Kravitz. His hand gripped Franzen's shoulder.

"Yeah, yeah. All right." But he wasn't. Chuck Franzen would never be all right. Of his eighty-four men, thirty-four were dead, twelve wounded. A fist full of dog tags dangling in front of him brought him back to reality. With a glassy stare, he took them, and then looked for someone to pass them off.

In an attempt to get Franzen talking, Roger Kahn squatted down to his eye level, "Lieutenant, how did you know to put the range at a thousand yards, we hadn't seen the guns yet?"

Staring at the ground, Franzen hesitated, then began to speak, "If they were at fifteen hundred yards, I didn't think we could hit them. If it was only five hundred, I figured they'd see us first and get us with direct fire. That left one thousand. I had a lot on my mind at the time. I don't know. Maybe just dumb luck.

---- Kahn?"

"Sir?" Kahn replied.

Franzen held out the bundle of dog tags, "Take these things,

I can't stand to touch 'em."

OOO

For forty plus years Chuck Franzen hid his bitterness. The senseless waste of his company festered in his heart. He didn't read about the war and wouldn't think of watching a war movie. When vets talked about their experiences, he would leave the conversation. He never joined the American Legion or attended any regimental reunions. The only things that could take him back to his painful memories were the events that surfaced now and again in his dreams. The one that appeared the most frequently was he staring at the long row of boots. Except for a strange ringing sound, the dream was always silent.

Christmas 1988
Teddy Franzen couldn't wait to give his granddad the present. He'd wrapped it in the Sunday comics, an old family tradition, and topped it with a red bow.

"Open it, Gramps. Open it."

Chuck slowly tore the paper away. Set the bow by his chair. No surprise, it was a book. The title shocked him a bit, however, "D-day Chronicles."

"Don't you like it, Gramps?" asked Teddy.

"Oh sure, I like it. You know I read a lot. Thanks, Teddy. It's a real nice present." He hugged his eldest grandson as long as he could and turned him loose.

Teddy gathered the wrappings, "You'll love it. It's all about D-day and how America won the war."

Chuck thumbed through the thick book glancing at photos, reading chapter titles, not yet sure he would ever read the book. Then, a chapter title caught his attention, "Rangers Secure Pointe du Hoc." The famous raid on the German artillery positions atop one hundred foot ocean cliffs grabbed his interest. The maps showed the point to be a short distance from the road to Formigny, the terrible road where Company-D was sent to its senseless destruction.

As the sounds of Christmas filled the house, Chuck delved deeper and deeper into the account. Oblivious to the Christmas music, the squealing grand kids, and the adult laughter, Chuck found the keys to a forty year old puzzle in the pages of Teddy's gift.

Page 109: *"German artillery shells, which were beginning to hit near the fortified area from somewhere inland--"*

"As they passed beyond the fortified area, some artillery and mortar shells began to drop near them."

Page 110: *"They began to meet artillery fire coming in salvos of three."*

"German artillery, estimated as light (75's or 88's) were searching the area with time fire,--"

Again and again, the German artillery, firing from somewhere inland, stalked the beleaguered rangers who held this critical strong hold and western hinge pin of Omaha Beach.

Page 122: *"At approximately 16:15 the artillery and mortar fire originating from inland mysteriously ceased."*

Chuck remembered the time when Warthogs-one and four delivered their attack; it was identical. The reason for Company-D's sacrifice jumped at him from page 122. It was no longer senseless, the lives no longer wasted.

Tears filled Chuck's eyes. His throat constricted with emotion. He tried to hide behind the book, but Teddy was watching. "What's wrong, Grampa?"

Chuck couldn't talk. Instead he motioned Teddy to follow him. Stopping at the roll-top desk in the den, he dried his eyes on his shirt sleeves. From the right side drawer, a leatherette case emerged.

"I want you to have this," as he handed it to his grandson.

"What is it?" Teddy asked.

The only thing Chuck could think of to say, "It's your

inheritance."

The boy's eyes grew larger as he opened the box, inside a Silver Star with a red, white and blue ribbon.

2 January 1989

Teddy Franzen straightened the black and gold frame; stepped back to see if it was level on his bedroom wall, then smiled with satisfaction as he read aloud.

"For conspicuous gallantry above and beyond the call of duty, this award is presented to First Lieutenant Charles D. Franzen, United States Army, who on 6 June, 1944 led an assault against a strategically located enemy artillery and mortar position north of Formigny, France.

Although sustaining heavy casualties in the initial phase of the attack, Lt. Franzen pressed forward to gain a better vantage point. Then with accurate cannon fire from his only two remaining tanks, destroyed said positions, thus aiding in the securement of an expanded beach head and the saving of untold numbers of American lives.

His heroism and dedication to duty is in keeping with the highest standards of the American military services.

Omar N. Bradley

Lt.General, US Army

Teddy's mother overheard the recital, and leaned into the room, "Your grandad was a real war hero, wasn't he?"

Teddy nodded, thought for a moment, "Shoot, he was my hero before I found out about this."

FOURTEEN

AN UNLIKELY REPLACEMENT

December 1944, Belgium

The morning fog seemed to hang in one place, unmoving, unchallenged. From his foxhole, Pfc. Melvin Silver could see nothing beyond twenty feet. Cold gripped his feet as it had all night, and his sore throat forecast the symptoms of a bad cold.

At home he would have had the unfailing attention of a Jewish mother - chicken soup, ancient family remedies and a warm bed. But there in the Ardennes Forest, in a hole in the ground, his misery was unabated.

Six months earlier, he'd stood on the high school stage to accept his diploma. Graduation night he didn't go out and get drunk like some of his class mates. He stayed home and tinkered with his short wave radio. Seven days after being assigned to B-company from the "repel depel," Melvin found himself in a shooting war. The frozen, crumpled corpses he'd seen the day before served as a grim reminder. Even Tony

101

Moretti, the man in the foxhole with him, seemed to be a fixture in a scene he didn't want to admit was real.

At a hundred and thirty-five pounds and five feet six, he wasn't anybody's poster boy. Confused and disillusioned, he was still trying to answer his own questions. *Why am I here? Why is this oversized automatic rifle assigned to me? Or am I assigned to it? Why are we out in the cold every night instead of in those houses back there? Jeez, I'm Jewish. If the Krauts capture me, I'll go to one of those labor camps. I hate physical work. Why me? Why?*

"The fog's kinda thick. Maybe the Krauts won't attack because they can't see either," Moretti murmured, but talking to no one but himself.

Melvin was shocked at the logic, "No, that's precisely when they will attack, when we can't see them. They, on the other hand, probably have seeing eye dogs, big Alsatians trained to devour Jews."

Moretti laughed, stroked his grubby beard, "I hope they know the difference between Italians and Jews. Maybe Mussolini negotiated a deal with Hitler."

Silence prevailed as Moretti munched on some kind of a K-ration, a weird orange bar which Melvin had never seen before. "What's that, pressed salmon ?" he asked.

"Yeah, that's it, pressed salmon with capers and hollandaise sauce. How did you know?"

Moretti looked at the B.A.R. next to Melvin, "How did you get the lieutenant to carry your rifle yesterday?"

Melvin sighed briefly, "I'm the lightest man in the platoon, why should I carry this woolly mammoth which turns my shoulder purple?"

Moretti stood up, stamped each foot a few times for circulation, "Do you always answer a question with another question?"

Melvin squinted, snuffed his runny nose and swallowed hard against his ailing throat, "Well okay. Let's see. I really wasn't finished with this B.A.R. thing. It weighs seventeen pounds, almost twice the M-1 rifle which you carry. That's nine and a half pounds. You, the hundred and eighty-five pound meatball from Hoboken, have a man to gun ratio of nineteen point five. I, on the other hand, have an MTG ratio of only seven point nine. The lieutenant weighs two hundred and his carbine only six and a half pounds, thus an MTG of thirty point something. And now you know the answer to your question."

"Sorry I asked," Moretti replied with a smirk.

"The fog is beginning to lift, maybe they won't need the dogs," Melvin quipped. As he straightened his helmet, another thought occurred to him. "These helmets need a chin strap, not a neck thing. Damn thing's always falling off."

Moretti shook his head in dismay, "I'll take it up with Ike, when next we dine together. Oh, there's one other thing. You ought to forget the phrase, *Why me*, or *why this* and *why that*, because all of these guys are just as sick of this war as you are. They don't care if you're cold, tired, or hungry. They don't care if the Krauts' big Alsatian dogs devour you and shit you out on the newly driven snow."

Melvin knew it didn't do any good to gripe to Moretti, but he still felt better venting his frustrations. He could see that his buddy was enjoying the satisfaction of his last retort. Melvin held it as long as he could, and then blurted out a hearty laugh. Moretti smiled, nodded his approval, his large white teeth gleaming.

The refuge of silence that followed, stimulated the visions of home, "Cold roast beef, horse radish, fresh rye bread, egg cream,... God, what I wouldn't do for an egg cream." For the first time in his life, he realized that he missed the serenity of Saturday temple, and the warmth of Sunday's family dinner. Still more, he missed the laughter, the singing and even Uncle Albert's violin.

A voice from behind him shook him from his thoughts, "Get ready, boys, Krauts a comin'." Platoon sergeant Harry Whittaker scurried from hole to hole, repeating the ominous warning.

Sounds seemed to come from every direction. They floated through the fog amplified further by Melvin's imagination. "Jeez, it sounds like a whole damned panzer division, and we're one under manned infantry company," he said aloud.

Ahead, an open field of white snow and white fog, he couldn't see a thing. Soon, the roar of powerful engines drowned out the other noises. Then three half tracks burst into view, their upper armor swirling the fog.

Immediately following the half tracks, Melvin could see German infantry men, clothed in white tunics and helmet covers. They were now only two hundred yards away. The fog was lifting.

The sounds grew louder, more ominous and yet not a single shot had been fired. "Hold your fire," a voice rang out. Closer pushed the enemy. As though someone threw a switch, the fog swirled and evaporated exposing the entire enemy unit.

"FIRE!"

The middle half track erupted in flames as a bazooka round struck its engine. The rocket's white smoke hung in place like a sky writer's trail, then disappeared in a gust of wind. A din of small arms erupted. Incoming rounds zinged everywhere, striking trees, the ground and the head logs around the foxholes.

Twenty yards to Melvin's left, a .30 caliber machine gun chattered short bursts, one after the other. B- Company was firing everything it had. On the open field, some Germans fell. Others scurried for the cover of the half tracks.

"Fire that goddamn thing Silver," Tony Moretti shouted.

"Oh, yeah, ah ..... fire." Melvin replied as he raised the BAR to the firing position. As if in slow motion, he worked the bolt, released the safety, squinted his left eye. "Damn, ice on the front sight."

"Fire that goddamn thing, Silver, or I'm gonna beat ya' over the head with it." Moretti continued to fire. A clip spring popped from his M-1 rifle. As he took another clip from the bandoleer, his face flushed with anger. Turning towards Melvin, he continued screaming, large purple veins bulging on his neck.

In Melvin's mind, the sounds of battle and Moretti's screaming fell silent. Although his ears failed him, his eyes saw a dangerous development. Seeking to outflank the American position, some enemy soldiers hustled towards the left. Again he squinted his left eye and prepared to fire, and again he stopped. He couldn't remember if his weapon was on "full auto" or "single fire." Flipping the receiver over , he was satisfied he had "full auto."

With his weapon tightly shouldered, Melvin finally fired his first shots in anger. The heavy *Thud, thud, thud, thud*, of his BAR broke the silence of his mind. His shoulder jerked with each shot. Germans dashed past Melvin as they fired at the nearby.30 caliber machine gun. *Thud, thud, thud, thud*, Melvin fired, shells tearing into his targets, red blotches contrasting on the white tunics, bodies tumbling.

His mind was a blank, but the BAR continued to fire as retreating Germans ran for cover. Melvin positioned another clip of ammo. Each target topped his sight. Each burst followed the path of his tracers, until the targets disappeared into the forest, and his rifle bolt bounced open.

Condensation from his rapid breathing had fogged his glasses. He could no longer see. Someone yelled, "Cease fire." Slowly, Melvin removed the glasses and wiped the lenses with a handkerchief. He then blew his nose with four short snorts. Still panting, he looked to his right. Moretti was seated at the bottom of the foxhole. His helmet held loosely between his chest and legs. Steam rose from his short, close cropped head of hair. A cigarette dangled precariously from his lower lip. "What the hell were you thinking?" he said. "You've got major fire power in your hands, and you sit there in a fucking trance."

Melvin slumped to the same sitting position, " I dunno. I

guess I got excited, er.... rather confused. That was my first action. You know something, Moretti, if the fog stayed for ten minutes more. Well, it could have been nasty."

Moretti took a drag on his cigarette, paused after exhaling, "I hope those two guys with the .30 caliber machine gun are okay. I'm afraid to look. Your 'er- confusion' may have caused them a lot of grief."

Using the BAR as a crutch, Melvin stood up , stepped from the foxhole, "Only one way to find out." With every step, the fresh snow crunched beneath the treads of his rubber boots.

In a minute, he returned. Moretti was still in the same position, still puffing on his cigarette, when Melvin slid back. "They're okay. One of 'em said thanks for dropping those three Krauts. He said his name was Greavy or Creasy or something like that."

"Greavy is right, Silver. The other guy is Cooper. You should get to know them. You may need them some day. "What three Krauts?" Moretti added as an after thought.

Melvin pointed, "Those three, right there." His bare hand trembling as he did. Quickly, he withdrew his hand, not sure if the tremble was from being scared or cold for he qualified for both.

As Moretti peered over the top of the foxhole, "Goddamn, Silver, you're a real hatchet man. I wouldn't have believed it ten minutes ago. Put your gloves back on."

That afternoon, the enemy attacked again, and was repulsed again; but B-Company was low on ammunition, medical supplies and the wounded were in need of attention. The Company-CO decided to evacuate their position on the ridge and try to find regimental headquarters.

Harry Whittaker returned to the position where Silver and Moretti sat shivering. Nightfall was only thirty minutes away. "Does anybody know anything about radios?" he asked.

"I do," replied Melvin. "I'm a short wave ham. What do you want to know?"

Whittaker squatted down close to the foxhole, "Our radio man was killed in the last attack, and we can't make contact with regiment and don't know where the hell they are."

Minutes later, Melvin was seated in front of the company's only remaining radio. The cover removed, he delved into its guts. "Put this battery under your coat," he said to the man next to him. Pvt. Gene Cascone did as he was told, "Is this gonna help? Damn thing's cold."

"That's part of the problem", Melvin replied. "The battery's low, we don't have a spare, and we don't have a good enough antenna. Also, I think I can play musical chairs with some of these tubes and get a better transmission. Luckily, the worst tube here has a spare taped to the inside of the housing. Your previous radio man did something right."

Cascone studied the red haired, skinny character in front of him, "Are you from Staten Island? You look familiar."

Melvin looked surprised, Cascone didn't look at all familiar to him. "Yeah, I'm from the Island. How did you know?"

"You worked in Silver's Deli, right?"

"Yeah, that's my father's place."

Cascone smiled broadly, "I used to buy chopped liver sandwiches there. Not for me, I hated 'em. My dad liked 'em though. He liked 'em with purple onion and rye bread. Sometimes he'd get Limburger and onion, and then get the farts. Your bagels were good though. "

Preferring to work on the radio, Melvin didn't react to Cascone's critique of the chopped liver. "I can only inspect these tubes visually and listen for rattles. I've moved some of the things and cleaned some contacts. I think it will help. Now for a better antenna. Do we have any wire we can run up a tree?"

Cascone reached into a metal ammo box, "Ya mean like this?"

Melvin's eyes lit up at what he saw, "Exactly like that."

Under the cover of darkness, Melvin scaled a tall, scrawny pine tree. The wire antenna he had fashioned looped over his shoulder. As he fixed the end of the antenna to a branch, a bullet skimmed through the tree, then another. "Holy shit," he cried, "The Krauts can see me."

Zzuht, zzhut, zzhut, bullets clipped the branches, clearing the snow from them in tiny, powdery blizzards. Hand over hand, foot over foot, Melvin made a hurried descent. The last six or eight feet turned into a free fall. "The Master Race can see at night, for Christ's sake," Melvin blurted as he dove into the nearest foxhole.

"No shit, sandwich boy, now get the hell off me," Cascone grumbled.

The shooting had stopped, when Melvin felt the pain in his right leg. "I think I've been hit," he said with a wince. His teeth clenched as the pain surged.

"Where is this million dollar hit, Silver?" asked Cascone.

"In my right leg, ...calf. Oh shit, it hurts."

With a bayonet, Cascone slit the pant leg of Mevin's trousers, "Hmmm, doesn't look good, Silver, but it ain't a wound. You just broke it from the fall. This would come under the heading of an injury, not a wound. No points. No purple heart. No hits, no runs and no errors, . Cascone smiled as he added, "one man left on base."

"You mean I don't get to go home?"

Cascone laughed, "Heh, heh, heh.... Silver wants to go home, guys. Did you hear that?" He shouted.

From out of the dark, the replies floated in sporadically:

"Take me with you, Silver."

"If his leg is broken, can we just leave him here?"

"Replacements. Shit, they just don't get it, do they?"

"Can I have your cigarettes, Silver? And the rubber boots too."

108

Sgt. Whittaker came crawling on all fours, "Silver, we just made contact with regiment. Your handy work paid off. We're pulling out in thirty minutes."

Cascone smiled, "Sarge, we got a problem. Hi- ho Silver here, just broke his leg. Who's gonna volunteer to carry him?"

"That's easy; Cascone, you and Moretti will carry him. Fixin' the radio may have saved the whole goddamn company. You can alternate with Greavy and Cooper. I'm sure they'll remember who saved their asses this morning. We're not leaving any wounded or injured, just malcontents and whiners."

Cascone smiled a half hearted smile, "You know me, Sarge, always there with a helping hand."

OOO

In 1964, Melvin Silver addressed the regimental reunion at Fort Drum, New York.

I am convinced that nothing happens without the hand of God. There is a reason for everything and nothing is by chance. It was the will of God that I go into the Army in 1944, that I trained and went to Europe to join B-company. At the time I could see no reason for any of it. I grumbled constantly. Ask Moretti.

Although my time with the company was barely three weeks before I was sent back to England, I helped fulfill God's plan for you and for myself. My acquired knowledge of radios helped the company to find its way back to safety.

Other units in that terrible battle did not, and were swallowed whole by the enemy.

"Why", I asked myself, was I there? Why did I have to carry that beast of a weapon called a B.A.R.? Why was it so damned cold? Why me? Why?

And now I know the answers to all of these. .....Because God wanted B-Company to live to fight another day. Because God wanted Greavy and Cooper to raise families. Because God wanted Melvin Silver to appreciate his family, his home and the United States of

America.

Twenty seven men from B-Company died in the service of our country. In cemeteries in Europe and the U.S., twenty-five crosses and two stars of David bear their names. Most of them I never knew, because I was a replacement. I have their names on this list before me, and a similar list at home. I am Jewish, but I believe in a life here after, so I pray for them nearly every day.

Do you know who I replaced in the foxhole with Tony Moretti? I did some checking. His name was Arnold Friese from New Jersey. Do you know who the radio operator was who got killed December nineteenth of '44? His name was John Cutler from Pennsylvania. I was chosen by my superiors and by my God to fill their shoes. I hope that you will pray for them too.

Thank you for being here tonight, and God bless you all.

Melvin Silver ran a successful catering business in Manhattan until he retired in 1994. He lives in Port Charlotte, Florida. He has three children and six grandchildren. An American flag flutters from his front porch every day, not just on holidays.

FIFTEEN

THE BOMBS, THE FUSES AND THE SABOTEUR

1941 - An armaments plant near Pilsen, Czechoslovakia

C esmir Pelcic glanced up from his work bench, then quickly back. Even if the Nazi supervisor had seen him, the glance would have gone unnoticed. It was the next move which was risky.

Pelcic's nimble fingers pulled a straight pin from his sleeve, and pushed it through a series of concentric layers of wax paper and tin foil. With a small side cutter he snipped off the pin's head, and then pressed the hole closed with his finger nail. The pin head itself being the only connection to the sabotage, he swallowed it with a gulp. The pin could short out the firing condenser, rendering the fuse and its bomb harmless. And then again, maybe it wouldn't.

If his scheme worked, maybe a British family would survive the Blitz, maybe a ship and its crew would be spared. Maybe Germany would lose the war.

Maybe...

Asphaltic compound poured around the assembly soon hardened, holding the firing condensers and circuitry in place, and concealing Pelcic's handy work. The modified E1AZ fuse went into a metal pan with the rest. In ten short seconds, Cesmir Pelcic had risked his life, now for the twenty-first time. He wasn't even sure his method was good, but the three circuit fuse was difficult to disable, and he had to try something.

The modified fuse, boxed in cardboard with the unmodified ones, began a long journey, but not to England. It headed east, then north. On a series of trucks and trains, it traveled through Poland, Lithuania, Latvia, then came to rest at an airfield near Luga in northern Russia.

Luftwaffe Sergeant Heinz Kimmle tore open the box, looked closely at the E1AZ designations, and then threaded the cylinder into the fuse pocket of an SC500 grade III, a big powerful, 500 kg bomb. With a piece of chalk, he wrote "No delay." As an after thought, he scribbled another note in German, "We fight with God." "A message to the godless Bolsheviks," he thought.

Kimmle's assistant chuckled, then cranked the jack handle up and down several times. The thousand pounds of death and destruction lifted into the bomb rack of a Heinkle-111 aircraft. An hour later, the bomber was airborne. With a gloved hand, the bombardier threw the arming switches; a row of small green indicating lights illuminated. Pelcic's fuse headed for Leningrad at 13:00 hours. It was Sunday.

March 1, 1881 St. Petersburg, Russia
After several abortive attempts to kill Tsar Alexander II, a simple oxide fuse detonated a bomb beneath his carriage. Unhurt, the Tsar made a fatal mistake and stepped down from the carriage to help his injured coachman and an injured pedestrian. A second bomb thrown at his feet by Ignaty Grinevitsky, severed his legs and left him bleeding to death on the street.

On the site of the assassination, Alexander III erected a memorial to his late father. The Church of the Resurrection of Jesus Christ was begun in 1803 and completed fourteen years later. With 17th century Russian architecture, the church's seven spires reach heavenward. Large, impressive mosaics cover every inch of interior wall space, and jasper inlaid floors add to the splendor.

In this magnificent church occurred no weddings or baptisms, no Sunday or daily masses. Only weekly requiems and religious readings resonated through its finely tuned acoustics. It was a church without a congregation, beautiful, but without a soul.

Stalin closed the doors in 1923 and looters took their toll on the decor. The church became better known as "The Savior on Spilled Blood," or simply, "The Church of the Spilled Blood."

November, 1941 - Leningrad

As air raid sirens wailed, terrified civilians scurried for the protection of basements and storage cellars. The drone of twenty plus German bombers soon added to the hysteria, then the bombs. Low thumps from the southwest at first, then shattering blasts shook the ground. Anti-aircraft batteries, all too few of them, hammered at the seemingly immune bombers above.

Pelcic's fuse and its 500 kg bomb tumbled from the bay of the Heinkle. As it fell, a loud *swoosh* accompanied its end over end flight. At over 200 miles per hour, the missle struck a tall window on the main cupola of The Church of the Spilled Blood, and plunged into the beautiful inlaid jasper floor below. Pieces of jasper sprayed the colorful icons in every direction.

As the drone of bombers faded into the afternoon sky, time held its breathe. No ticking came from the bomb, but nobody could be reached to defuse it. The next day, the bomb had still not exploded. In Russian, German or any other language, it was called a *dud*.

May, 2003

Vadim, the friendly travel guide, said that God saved the Church of the Spilled Blood, and that's true. What he didn't say was that God's instrument of salvation was a thin, bony-faced Czech named Cesmir Pelcic.

Only God knows how many of Pelcic's straight pins prevented bombs from exploding. The three circuit electrical fuse was well designed and Pelcic's sabotage method imperfect. In October of 1999, thirteen years after Pelcic's death, British construction workers unearthed a big, huge 1000 kg bomb near the train line at Woodley, England. A faulty fuse was blamed, or praised, as the case may be.

Renovated in 1997, you can still visit The Church of the Spilled Blood. You can still travel to the little town of Woodley, near Reading. Somehow, in the realm of the twilight zone, the two are mysteriously linked. Cesmir Pelcic sleeps well in a place of peace and light, no medals on his chest, his courage known only to God.

Sixteen

Things That Go 'Bump' in the Night

December 1944, Belgium

J oachim Peiper was a striking figure in his black and silver SS uniform. A Reiter Kreuz dangled from a black and white ribbon at his throat, and an aura of arrogance permeated his persona. From the hatch of his Panther tank he looked eastward at the massive orange glow in the sky. "Now what?" he asked himself.

Still peering to the east, he keyed his radio mic, "Spearhead-one to spearhead-three, what is your disposition? Over." In reply he heard only static. Peiper cursed as he slapped his gloved hand on the hatch rim. Pain shot from his wrist as it hit the locking lug. "Goddamn it!" He cursed again.

Peiper knew his mission must be completed in seventy-two hours, by then the Americans would recuperate and the element of surprise wasted. Meanwhile his detachment of armor was stretched for petrol and he knew the explosion that lit up the night sky probably just made that element worse.

The Panther roared on through the night, the metal treads clanking noisily on the unpaved road. He had made this trip just ten days earlier to test the speed and fuel economy of the Panther, and the calculations were marginal at best. One small town after another shook with the weight and the thunder of the tanks, their objective- the Meuse River and the port of Antwerp.

British airfield near Dover

Lt. Jimmy Bowman (U.S. Army Air Corps) stared at the dimly lit runway in front of him, pushed both throttles to the wall and released the brakes. Twin 2000HP engines roared, fire shot from the exhaust ports. In seconds the P-61 night fighter lifted from the runway and into the pitch of a moonless, overcast night. It was the twelfth mission for Jimmy and his two man crew.

His oxygen mask hung unattached, since he wouldn't be going above ten thousand feet. He banked slightly to the right and took a heading of 090 degrees. Jimmy loved the P-61 and had affectionately named his bird "The Boogey Man." A large white skull with smiling teeth decorated the nose just aft of the plexiglas.

With four 20mm cannon, four .50 caliber machine guns, and the all important radar, "The Boogey Man" could break things and hurt people.... at night.

Once past the Channel, he took evasive action just for practice, chinking left, then right. Soon he was east of the Meuse River and headed north. But for the drone of the engines, silence gave way to his radar observer, Lt. Herman Sparks.

"Target up. Jimmy," he blurted into the intercom.

"What does it look like, Herm?"

"Six trucks in a wad, towing trailers, I think."

Before beginning his gunnery pass, Jimmy keyed his radio mic, "Boogey Man to Barnyard Base, come in."

The radio reply was instantaneous, "Barnyard Base, go

ahead Boogey Man."

"Somethin' is up in the Ardennes, Barnyard Base. We have truck convoy twenty miles southeast of La Gleize. We are attacking, now."

The night was no longer cold. Adrenalin rushed through Jimmy's body as he took a steep bank, 3-g turn and lined up on the road. Herman's even tempered directions calmed him, but the hills on either side of the road were unnerving to say the least. Things happened fast and before he knew it, Jimmy was holding down the trigger, three, four, five seconds. The flash from the guns lit up the cockpit, cannons thumping heavily. A long arch of tracers found the trucks, and one after the other exploded in a large orange fire ball. Soon the fireballs were as one rising a thousand feet, and glowing against the heavy overcast.

Pulling back on the stick, Jimmy felt the blood drain from his head. Tunnel vision dimmed the instrument panel in front of him. *Thump* went something in his right engine. In the dark he could not see the engine, but the tachometer was bouncing crazily, oil pressure fluctuating. It was going to be a long flight home.

At ten thousand feet he leveled off and immediately throttled back on the right engine. The white Cliffs of Dover would be a welcomed sight he thought to himself. Jimmy smiled, despite the peril, and then began singing, *"There'll be blue birds over the white Cliffs of Dover."*

Herman interrupted, "Jimmy, can we leave that one to Vera Lynn?"

"-tomorrow. Just you wait and see." Jimmy continued. The volume doubled when he reached his favorite verse, *"The shepherd will count his sheep. The valleys will bloom again, and Jimmy will go to sleep in his own little room again."* They both laughed when at last he'd finished all four verses, but quickly had to return to reality. A dip in the Channel in December was a sobering thought.

Although throttled back, the troubled right engine was beginning to vibrate noticeably. When he could no longer chance a fire, Jimmy shut it down and feathered the prop. The drone of the single engine made the return trip seem eternally longer, the stress doubled it yet again. Perspiration ran down his back and soaked his underarms, and yet his feet were cold.

Daylight crept slowly out of the clouds. It bounced off the white cliffs like a beacon. "Boogey Man to Barnyard Base, we're home. One pass only, one engine inoperative. Over."

"Barnyard Base- You're clear, Boogey Man."

The black painted P-61 rolled to a stop on a parking stand of pierced steel plank. With creaky limbs and sore butts, the crew climbed out and joined the crew chief as he examined the right engine. Perched atop a ladder, Sgt. Bill Moody was pulling pine limbs, cones and needles from the engine cowling. The prop was bent and a goodly dent glared from the leading edge of the wing. "Ya got a little low last night, Lieutenant. Better watch that."

Jimmy Bowman sighed, "Ya can't see everything, Moody. Flying a night fighter is a tough job even in daylight."

Moody looked at Sparks, "What did he say? Flying a night fighter in daylight? Jeez!"

Before Jimmy Bowman and the "Boogey Man" landed at Dover, the German artillery barrage had started. The Battle of the Bulge was just beginning and already Joachim Peiper was losing confidence in the plan. More disappointments were in store for him as American combat engineers blew one bridge after another and denied him passage to the Meuse.

Jimmy Bowman never knew that he fired the first shots of the greatest battle in American history, nor did he know how important they were.

Years later, when his grand children asked him what he did in the war, he answered briefly, "I flew a night fighter, a P-61 – it was one of those things that go 'bump' in the night. It wasn't any big deal."

Standartenfuhrer Joachim Peiper escaped the noose at Nuremberg although men in his command committed the massacres at Stavalot and Malmedy. To him the loss of his emergency fuel supply *was* a big deal. In an interview with American Stars and Stripes reporters in 1947, he said, "The most decisive moment in the battle occurred with the opening shots." Thirty years later he was killed by arsonists in a small town in France.

The irony of Jimmy Bowman's twelfth mission was that his radar found the fuel trucks and not Peiper's much larger armored column. The tactical value of the tanks would have been more attractive than the strategic value of the fuel trucks. Lost in the darkened, winter forest of the Ardennes, the fuel trucks could have fueled Peiper's spearhead.

SEVENTEEN

MIND GAMES

The Ardennes Forest, December 15, 1944

P vt. Henry Switzer wrestled with the duffle bag trying to load it with all of his belongings. Cans of Spam rolled to the floor with a noisy racket. His company mates grumbled.

They had a right to. The movie had run for ninety minutes and was nearing an uncertain ending. "Keep it down, Switzer," one guy bellowed. The movie ended with the usual circles, x's and numbers; and then the screen went white with blinding effect.

"What're ya doing, Hank?" asked Pvt. Olin Thrash.

Switzer looked up from his kneeling position, "I'm trying to prepare for the attack."

"What attack?" asked Thrash.

"Olin, I don't expect you to understand this, but we are in for a massive attack from the Krauts."

"How did you come to that conclusion, oh great swami?

Hey, aren't you a Kraut?"

Hank smiled, "The Germans haven't launched a winter attack since Frederick the Great. We haven't seen a German tank in nearly three months. Hitler is desperate to gain a cease fire and negotiate. He probably is arguing right now with his generals, but they will attack and probably right where they did in 1940, the Ardennes Forest. And yes, I am a Kraut. My parents were born and raised in Berlin. They came to the U.S. in 1922.They settled in Wisconsin. I was born two years later."

Olin rubbed the back of his head, "Hank, aren't we in the Ardennes now?"

"Brilliant, my boy, we are. That is why I've checked out these blankets, extra rations and even, God forbid, these emergency med kits."

With that, Hank rose to his feet, and stuck a bayonet through the center of a wool blanket. He ripped about twelve inches of material, then pulled it over his head. A wide cartridge belt wrapped his waist, tucking the blanket closer. "They didn't have any great coats, so this will have to do. Here, I got one for you."

As he slit the blanket, Olin asked, "Do you really think all this is necessary?"

"Not necessary if you want to freeze your butt off. I also checked out rubber goulashes, but they wouldn't give me two pair. I suggest you get over to supply and get some. It's snowing out already. Get extra socks too."

Reluctantly, Olin left and headed for the regimental supply depot, still scratching his head.

The next morning, as they finished breakfast, the regimental commander and his staff burst into the mess hall, "Mess hall, Atten-hut," shouted an aid. Colonel Ed March slapped his left hand with a swagger stick, "Men, we are being attacked by a large force of enemy soldiers, an artillery barrage is falling just twenty miles east of here. If you go outside, you can hear it.

Early reports indicate they have large numbers of tanks. We're in for a fight."

Across the room, Olin Thrash turned, searching for Hank. Their eyes met. Hank raised his eye brows as if to say, "See, I told ya so."

The colonel continued, we need help in G-2. Can anyone type? Can anyone speak German?"

Hank raised his hand, "Both, Sir."

Olin's hand was also raised, "Type yes; German no. Sir."

The colonel turned to an aid and whispered, "Get those two men over to G-2. Get the German speaker to monitor the radio transmissions. The typist, get him busy on that stack on my desk. I had a feeling in my gut somethin' was up." He stormed out of the mess just as he had entered. An aid shouted again, "Mess hall, Atten-hut."

An hour later, plans changed and the regiment loaded their trucks and headed for a small town south of Bastogne. In the crowded trucks, men grumbled, made jokes, and in desperation pitched out things they didn't want. Gasmasks, chairs, wooden crates and an occasional barf bag full of piss hit the roadside.

Within days of G-2 setting up in an old school building, reports were beginning to filter in that unarmed young German soldiers were drifting into American lines. The number was too great to be coincidental. "They weren't lost, they were cheap reconnaissance," concluded Switzer. His new C/O, a newly promoted captain from Louisiana, Beauregard "Bo" Tratteau, agreed. Something was strange about these unarmed privates. Usually very young, fifteen or sixteen, and all shaking in their boots with fear, all save one.

Pvt. Fritz Heilmann, 26th Volksgrenadiers appeared at a distance with other prisoners. Intuition gnawed at Switzer's psyche. "That guy sticks out like a sore thumb," he complained to the captain.

Tratteau hesitated, "How so?"

"That guy is older than the rest. He doesn't have military

bearing that would come just from their boot camp. He's always looking around, the others are all downcast. Sir, let me question him, in the office. Let me have an armed guard, but I need to appear as an officer. Do you still have your lieutenant's bars?"

The captain wrestled through the usual pocket junk and showed Switzer the bars. He grinned as he pinned them onto Switzer's shoulder epaulets. "Field commission; don't let it go to your head, Lieutenant."

Down the street, an artillery shell exploded lifting a deuce and a half truck onto its side. As the truck burned, nobody rushed to put it out. Fires had become commonplace. Choking, heavy smoke hung low over everything.

Switzer had just gotten comfortable at a desk when the guard bought Heilmann in, and placed him in front him. He never looked up at the prisoner, in crisp German he demanded, "Stand at attention in the presence of an officer."

Heilmann's heels clicked. His back straightened and his chin stuck out straight.

"Ja vol, Oberleutnant."

"Grenadier Heilmann, your papers indicate you are the lowest possible rank, and yet your uniform is new, your identity card is new, and you are older than that card indicates. How did you evade military service all this time, until now?"

"There are ways to serve the Reich other than in the military," responded Heilmann.

"You mean like in the Abwehr or the Gestapo?"

Heilmann stiffened; then relaxed his demeanor, "Those would be two options."

"Your identity card is brand new, no dog ears on the corners like all the rest out there. How do you account for that?"

Heilmann squirmed a bit but answered abruptly, "I lost my card a couple weeks ago and was issued a new one."

"You're from Berlin, are you not?

"No I am from Ulm, but then I am not supposed to reveal

that information according to the Geneva Convention." An artillery shell burst overhead, spraying the building with shrapnel. Heilmann flinched, bent at the knees. His left arm curled around his forehead. "This guy hasn't seen any combat," Switzer thought to himself.

"Herr Heilmann, do you speak any foreign languages?"

"I am Grenadier Heilmann, and I speak a smattering of several languages. My English is not very good."

Switzer was making small talk, but every response from Heilmann was telling him a little. Heilmann's arrogance alone was unbefitting a lowly grenadier. The questioning continued for an hour, but Heilmann was evasive, calculating. Switzer's last question, "Are you related to General Heilmann?"

"No. If I was, I would have a soft staff job in Berlin and be an officer." Switzer's blank countenance contrasted sharply with Heilmann's nervous laughter.

Switzer stacked a small pile of papers, "Guard, take this man to the portable holding cell. Separate him from all other prisoners, and post a twenty-four hour guard. He is to be treated as a level one prisoner."

Another shell exploded across the street. Voices yelled for help. It was four-thirty and already getting dark, and colder, and shells continued to fall.

Seated on crates, in what had been a storage room for the school, Captain Tratteau and Switzer talked. A blanket covered the window. The only light came from a flashlight tipped on its side and shining straight up. Bombs were falling on nearby Bastogne. The building trembled. Dust fell from the rafters.

Switzer chewed on a K-ration dehydrated fruit bar, "I'm concerned that this Heilmann is on a mission. He has a timetable, and he's running out of time. He may try something soon, either escape or getting to one of our own radios."

"From everything you've told me, he probably is and will try something, but what?" Tratteau responded.

"He says he's from Ulm, but he speaks like a Berliner. Only recently entered the army, so he probably was in the Abwehr. He was not the least bit frightened when first captured, so he was where he wanted to be. He wanted to learn something about us, our morale or our equipment." Switzer paused, his mind raced back to the truck ride, the gas masks and junk lining the road. "The gas masks," he blurted.

Switzer's eyes enlarged with what he had just concluded. He stood up, staring at the captain, "Hitler will use nerve gas if he can't take Bastogne. He wants to know if we all have gas masks."

Tratteau lit a cigarette, "Do you think he would risk opening that can o'worms? The Allies would never negotiate with him if he did."

Switzer countered, "Hitler must be desperate, fighting on two fronts, being bombed day and night. If he thinks there is no chance at negotiation, he'd gas everybody in Bastogne to break through to Antwerp. It must be one of his options, and he's waiting for word from Heilmann. Which is why Heilmann can't go anywhere or talk to anyone."

Switzer removed the .45 automatic from his holster, and walked briskly to the adjacent classroom. Captain Tratteau following on his heels, "Switzer, don't do anything rash. I'm warning you. Don't do it."

As Switzer opened the classroom door, Heilmann scrambled to shoulder the guard's rifle. Switzer fired. Fired again, and then a third time. Heilmann twisted and turned with each shot. The heavy slugs knocked him backwards and knocked him dead. His bright blue Aryan eyes stared blindly at the ceiling.

The opened brass padlock lie on the floor next to an unconscious guard. Protruding from the brass lock, a paper clip sat unraveled. It's inside loop all that showed. The guard stirred, held his head like he had the worst hangover of his life, and moaned, "Oh my God. What the hell happened?"

Tratteau bent over Heilmann's lifeless body, "He's dead. No

126

question about it." He looked up at Switzer, "Would you have done it if he hadn't tried to escape?"

Switzer bit his lower lip, "What the hell do you think?"

March 30ᵗʰ, 1945, Ramagen, Germany

Henry Switzer wore the bars of a real lieutenant as he drove across the pontoon bridge. The jeep bounced with every seam in the planking. The old Ludendorf Bridge, no longer structurally sound, stood parallel a quarter mile up river to the north. He had just crossed when he heard a familiar voice, "Lieutenant, Lieutenant Switzer, over here." A familiar face went with the voice, Pvt. Olin Thrash. With a grin on his face, "Come with me, Hank."

The cave was large and deep. Water dripped from the roof, wetted the floor. A stack of wooden coffins sat to one side, perhaps eighty or so. Thrash continued on, then turned right into a smaller, narrower cave. "Here it is. We found it yesterday."

Switzer gazed at the stack of crates, each marked in German, 'ARTILLERY 88MM SOMAN.'

"You were right after all, Lieutenant. I gotta admit. I had my doubts. I guess that's why you're an officer and I'm still a private. That Soman is bad shit. Ain't it?"

July 1945, Berlin, Abwehr HQ, 76 Tirpitzufer, Berlin

Switzer squinted in the dimly lit archives. The endless personnel files and the bad lighting were straining his eyes. He sneezed for the essence of mildew had already entered the unheated file room. "Hallman, Herman, Hiller, no Heilmann. Damn." Switzer's frustration grew as he looked further and further into the musty files. Another drawer, fifty more files and nothing. He considered quitting when a photograph slipped from the last file in the stack. The subject was stern faced, defiant, dressed in a wool suit and silk tie. The file said Zimmerman, Karl O., but it was Heilmann.

Zimmerman's long service record unfolded in front of Switzer. Spain 1938, Poland 1939, France 1940, "A regular tourist," Switzer said to himself. Carefully, he read the dossier to the last entry- "Op # 37890 die Wacht am Rhein- tote."

"Yes. Zimmerman was *tote*, in the Battle of the Bulge. His Soman was in a cave in Ramagen, and my gas mask went out the tailgate like everybody else's."

Eighteen

One-eyed Jack

April 22, 1945, Berlin

Bombs were falling a few kilometers away as Joachim Hutzler watched the last four Bf-109's race down the runway. "But that was only three," he said to himself. Where is the fourth?"

Hutzler dashed from the operations shack to see a lone Messerschmitt on the tarmac, the prop spinning, its engine idling. The cockpit was empty. Beyond the aircraft, the pilot crouched on all four's retching, his parachute and leather helmet in a heap nearby. A mechanic offered, "He's got the flu. Been up most of the night heaving."

Hutzler hadn't flown in nearly five years, but the urge was overwhelming. With one hand he scooped up the parachute, the helmet with the other. As he ran, he fastened the clasps at chest and legs. In a minute he was on the wing and into the cockpit. Quickly he released the static bar that locked the controls. It fell to the floor with a metallic *clang*. The aircraft began taxiing while Hutzler wrestled with the leather helmet and oxygen mask. Two mechanics followed at a gallop shouting, "Major, don't do it. Major, stop. You'll get into trouble, Major." The roar of the engine drowned their pleas, and the modeled grey fighter turned onto the runway. Light rain pelted the windscreen and made little rings in the puddles on the pavement. Hutzler pushed the throttle full forward, felt the tail wheel lift. As he pulled back on the stick, he was filled with a rush he hadn't felt since he first soloed that old trainer back in 1938. It was exhilarating. The runway markers sped past, liftoff!

The gear came up, and then the flaps. Hutzler screamed into his mask as five years of pent up emotions, five years of frustration and anger bellowed from his vocal chords. *Yeee-hawww!*

Tears welled in his eye, for he only had one. A black patch covered the socket where the other once resided. Instantaneous flashbacks passed through his mind, the old Henschel-123 fighter-bomber with double wings, the tracers chewing up the three Soviet I-16's. The beautiful, dark eyed Spanish girl, "What was her name? Magda, Magda, Magdalena. Ja, Magdalena."

The crash in 1940 then loomed like a bad dream. It was only his third flight in a Bf-109 when a gust of wind lifted his left wing. The right one hit the runway just before touchdown. It could not have been more untimely. As the beautiful fighter ground looped, it tore to pieces. A canopy strut punctured his goggles and his eye. He awoke in a hospital the next morning. A doctor stared down at him, "You're lucky to be alive."

"Some luck," Hutzler responded.

With the flip of a switch, alcohol and water injected into his supercharger. Even as he throttled back a bit, he felt the added thrust of the alcohol. "If I don't catch up to the others in three minutes, I'll be all alone up here." He passed thru five-thousand meters as he turned off the alcohol injector and throttled back. "Green four to green one, come in," he said into the microphone. Silence. "Green four to green one, over." More silence. The radio freq was written on the back of his hand, and it checked correct on the radio dial. "Why doesn't he answer?"

The day dreams ended. His hands were cold, incredibly cold. "Where are your gloves, Jochy?"

The cloud cover was dissipating. To the south, formations of American bombers were loosing their bombs. Hutzler began calculating his best attack. Attacking the rear formation made sense. Maybe they wouldn't get the chance to drop their bombs. He would attack at their six o'clock, and hold the trigger until the ammo was gone, a split-s and head for home.

"God, help me," he whispered as he threw the arming switches on the guns. With another switch he let the belly fuel tank drop away. Quickly the 109 jogged left, and then right as Hutzler cleared his rear. He swallowed hard, "Here goes nothing. Five years of war and I get ten seconds of it."

Just then, below and to the right, four FW-190's appeared, flying right to left at almost ninety degrees. Directly behind them, no less than eight P-51's.were closing. "Green four to flight of 190's north of Frankfurt, JG-76 watch your tail. Alarm, alarm." The JG-76 was a calculated guess, but the warning had no effect. Frantically, he switched to emergency frequency, repeating the same warning, again, to no avail.

The friendly aircraft heard nothing, did nothing. The Mustangs were closing, almost within firing range. Hutzler rolled into a diving turn to the left. When his gun sight was out ahead of the lead P-51, he pressed the trigger. Well out of range, but it didn't matter. The tracers arched down in front of the Mustangs as Hutzler worked his rudder pedals back and forth. To the mustang pilots it must have looked like a whole squadron was attacking them from above. The Mustangs broke, four to the left and four to the right.

Finally, the 190's realized their peril and began taking evasive action. The leader looked back just in time to see a lone Messerschmitt disappear into a cloud bank, two Mustangs in hot pursuit. He laughed aloud as he pressed his radio button, "Ha, ha, ha. Gentlemen, you have just witnessed a guardian angel. Don't ever disbelieve in them. Deny your god and you are a stupid atheist. Deny the guardian angels and you are insane."

Hutzler's aircraft buffeted as he entered the cloud. One last look over his left shoulder told him he was in trouble. The P-51's were menacing, six .50 caliber guns, faster and capable of out turning him.

In the middle of the cloud, he rolled up side down, and pulled back on the stick. In an instant he was out of the cloud and headed for mother earth. Leveling out at a thousand meters, his neck strained to see if his pursuers were following. There were none. He could only turn left where the good eye could see. The handicap of the missing eye became very evident. In a series of left's Hutzler made it home to his home base. As his aircraft rolled to a stop, mechanics slid chocks beneath the tires, and then stood back and applauded with smiles and clapping hands. Others gathered to do the same, including the three pilots he could not find in the cloudy skies over Germany.

Days later, the bombing campaign ended. Four young pilots lived to remake Germany, and Joachim Hutzler went back to Dortmund to write books, teach school and raise a family.

March, 1961
The new Bundeswehr Luftwaffe celebrated the nomination of a new commander at a dinner reception in West Berlin. Joachim Hutzler in civilian suit, tie and blue oxford clothe shirt attended. He could see his old friend and Condor Legion mate, Adolf Galland at the speakers table. Among such luminaries as Bubi Hartmann, Mackey Steinhoff and Gerd Barkhorn, Hutzler was unknown and unnoticed.

His dark hair now graying, his thin physique still thinner, Hutzler sipped his wine, enjoyed the dinner and listened to a host of speeches. Finally, the new commander spoke. He challenged the new Luftwaffe to dedicate themselves to perfection. Extolled them to build a new Germany as a freedom loving democracy, and then slipped into the nostalgia of his war time experiences. Finally recounting his last mission, "Over the radio, I told my men, 'Gentlemen; you have just experienced a guardian angel. Don't ever disbelieve in them. If you deny your god you are a stupid atheist, but if you deny a guardian angel, you are insane.' If I knew who he was, I would toast him tonight and I would hug him around his neck. The general lifted his glass. To my guardian angel."

"Hear, hear," chimed the assembly.

From the back of the banquet hall, came a voice, "Herr General, das wurde ich, derjenige angestarrter Wegeheber sein." ("Herr General, that would be me, the One-eyed Jack.") The general smiled, raising his glass in toast, bidding the stranger closer. The hall brimmed with laughter.

"Come forward, my friend. Was it you who was my guardian angel on the 22nd of April?"

Hutzler stood at his place, his back ramrod straight, "Herr General. *You* were my only mission."

133

NINETEEN

EVER THIS DAY

Luxembourg. January, 1945

The young soldier was on the edge of consciousness, and mumbling. Lt. Anne Hardaway leaned closer to hear what he was saying. "Angel of God, commit me here, ever this day be at my side." The words slurred, and then stopped altogether.

She felt his pulse. His eyes opened, "Are you an angel?" He asked with a whisper.

What he saw was brown eyes with long lashes, beautiful lips with a medium shade of lipstick, and a clear complexion. Her hair was tucked inside of a surgical cap, but it was auburn. A hank of it looped from the front of the cap, a muted fashion statement. The only jewelry, a gold crucifix, hung from a chain squeezed sideways between two dog tags

"No, you're not there, soldier. You're in a surgical hospital near Luxembourg City." We took some shrapnel out of your head and some from your shoulder. You're doing fine."

The words were comforting, but the sight of a woman so close did more for Pvt. Ethan Wills than the penicillin that coursed through his newly modified veins. He could smell her perfume, light, like those white flowers that grew on the hedge in his mother's garden. He grasped her hand, squeezed tightly. His face wrinkled, "Don't leave me."

"I'll be back in a few minutes. Others are just now coming out of the OR." His grasp lightened, and then her hand slipped away. Sleep returned in seconds.

Anne Hardaway stood up. Only then did she realize how much blood had spilled upon her white surgical gown. She wondered how many types were there, O, B, AB, A? Which Rh factors? "Why is that an issue? I'm so tired."

Twelve hours had passed since she changed, twenty four since she slept. Her mind was swimming. A hundred young faces flashed before her,- muddy, bloody, torn, once handsome, now some disfigured, some no longer alive. Ashen complexions, never to take the color of flesh revolted her. The smell of ether gnawed at her, flipping her stomach, filling her saliva with salt. She fought off the nausea, hoping nobody was watching. Then tears and the gripping at the throat, she fought them off too. Bit her lip, "Back to work." Her eyes squeezed shut, like the sights would never return once opened. She was wrong. A new litter lowered before her, and again the same scenario. The ticket called for penicillin, further cleaning especially around the wound. "God, what an awful wound."

She was almost finished when she realized her new patient was semi-conscious. He was watching her, and smiling. She smiled back. Pointing to his own eye as if to say "You look like.." and then "Rita Hayworth" issued from his lips.

Anne blurted out a laugh, "Not on my best day, buddy." She continued smirking, the compliment, though an exaggeration, was like a shot of vitamin B-12. "Angel of God, then Rita Hayworth, what'll these guys come up with next? I'll probably look like somebody's mother. Now there's a turn off."

From a small envelope, she shook three vitamin tablets, chased them with a gulp of water. She looked around the room, hoping again that nobody noticed. The questions might start again. Everybody, not just the delirious patients, was remarking on her rosy complexion. The weight gain was there too. Not as easily explained away by vitamins, cans of Spam or clean living.

OOO

Her head hit the pillow at 07:00. Sleep hit her head at 07:01. In minutes she was into a dream, standing on a hill, winds gusting, snow swirling about her. Visibility was poor, but she could see Mike on another hill. He was running, his platoon running behind him all bunched up. "Spread out, you guys, keep your interval," she shouted. Her warning came out as a series of muffled blather no one could have deciphered. To her horror, shells began exploding all around the platoon. Anne screamed. Her eyes opened and she found herself sitting on the edge of her cot, tears welling, spilling onto her cheeks.

"You all right, Anney?" asked her friend Libby Foster.

"Yea, yea, all right. I had a bad dream. It's the third time."

"Third time of what," asked Libby.

"It's the third time I've dreamed of Mike. He's always under fire, never sitting around talking or drinking a cup of coffee, never near me, always at a distance. He's always being shot at by heavy stuff. The dream is always in black and white, like a newsreel or movie."

Just then the buzzer went off calling them both to duty. It was 09:00. "Two hours sleep, Anne muttered. "I guess we get overtime now, right?"

Libby responded,"Yeah, two times nothin' is still nothin'

OOO

At the operating table instead of post op, Anne felt bolstered by the sleep, a bowl of oatmeal and her coffee. And the parade of sleeping faces passed by her until she no longer could see differences. They all had the same look, like boys at her brother's military school. Hundreds of them paraded by, and at a distance, all very much the same. When possible, as they moved each soldier, she kissed him on the forehead. Others she tenderly closed their eyes, never again to open. But never did she fail to say a prayer for a patient she touched. "Lord, give him healing or a happy death," the most common.

OOO

St. Joseph's Hospital, Atlanta, Georgia May 1945
Anne Hardaway finished nursing the newborn infant, and then kissed him gently. Her eyes followed the blue blanket bundle as the nurse took him back to the nursery. Loneliness had taken residency in her tiny patient room, her parents gone, her brother on the West Coast with his family. She had nobody,"Maybe someday, the child," she mused.

In her drifting mind, she pictured Mike, so handsome in his uniform, the restaurant in London, walks by the Thames...all gone now. The photo of the military cemetery at Hamm, Luxembourg sat in her purse, the corner protruded past the snap. A colorless photo belied the fact that a new lawn was, at that very moment, springing where Mike found his final resting place.

Anne knew the post-partum depression was a part of it, but wondered if life would ever be the same. She tried to sip from the straw in the water glass, but it sucked like the bottom of a milk shake that's not ready to give up. "Life wasn't fair and she had better get use to it," she thought. Discharged from the Army, her only fault had been that she fell in love during wartime. She brushed a tear from the corner of her eye, sniffed to stop a runny nose.

Through the hospital's ambient noise came a voice,"Miss Hardaway, Anne Hardaway? You'll never guess how I found you. Your friend Libby…Well, ah, er.. You probably don't remember me. My name is Ethan Wills.

Anne smiled, and through her dried and cracked lips, "- ever this day be at my side."

Ethan's hand trembled, "I brought you these flowers."

Twenty

P.O.W.

December 19, 1944 the Ardennes

Darkness was settling over the snowy landscape when Lt. Col. Joe Puett decided he would make a break for it. Nothing but trouble could come of going to a Stalag back in Germany. Because of the large numbers of prisoners, the Germans had not yet taken his name, rank and serial number. He was a P.O.W. because he was ordered to surrender, but now he was bound by the Military Code of Justice to attempt escape.

The small area surrounded by a single strand of barbed wire was crowded with dispirited Americans. Their weapons gone, their faces reflected the awful depression that had set in since the mass surrender of nearly the entire 106th Infantry Division. No longer was there a sparkle in their eyes, no joking or teasing. For most of them, this had been the worst day of their young lives.

A few puffed on cigarettes. None had any food, nor had they for three days. Those with wounds had no pain killers or even clean bandages. All of this and darkness would soon bring the cold.

Joe Puett watched intently at the handful of guards. Mostly boys and older men of the Volks Grenadiers had been assigned the duty. Hardened SS troopers would be a different deal. "These guys will be as sleepy as we are come sunset," he thought.

Soon he was gazing at a darkened overcast sky, no moon and the wind was picking up. Darkness fell quickly. His plan called for crawling on his belly under the wire and then to the nearby woods forty or fifty yards distant. Once in the woods, he'd stand up and walk slowly to the south. Joe cussed the compass he'd lost on the first day of the battle, it was part of the reason he found himself in this predicament. His first sergeant had replaced it and now the new compass would be essential for his escape. Joe snickered to himself as he remembered the compass was an official Boy Scouts of America model, not GI issue.

The snow and ice pushed through the top of his overcoat; it found ways into his sleeves and over the top of his boots as he crawled. Soon he was chilled worse than before. When he reached the woods, he looked back. Nobody was following; in fact he couldn't see any of the guards. As planned, he stood up and walked deeper into the woods. From his coat lining, he pulled the compass held by a safety pin, and turned slightly to head southward. In the distance he heard heavy artillery, and wondered whose.

The melting snow had soaked his clothing through to his skivvies, and it was too late to be opening things up to dry. Slowly he proceeded, hoping he wouldn't stumble into a German patrol. The new snow crunched beneath his leather G.I. boots. They too were soaked. The boots got cussed. The cold, the wet, the Germans, the surrendering, the dark, everything got cussed as only Joe could cuss it.

For a solid hour Joe walked before hearing a sound other than the wind and creaking trees. He stopped in his tracks when he realized it was the German language he was hearing.

Crouching down, he duck walked to a swale surrounded by windfall tree limbs. Ten yards ahead a column of Germans trudged on a trail ninety degrees to Joe's march.

In the darkness, he probably would never have seen them but for the white helmet covers and ponchos. Every fourth or fifth man carried a machine gun, the barrels bobbed as they walked. No silence routine was being observed as they talked freely, and Joe thankful for that. Then he thought, if I had just one company, I could ambush that lot and finish them all. But he was alone and unarmed, and lucky to evade detection.

At ten o'clock Joe came upon a farm house and small barn. The roof had been blown off the house, but the barn was intact. Joe approached cautiously. No smoke came out of the stacks, no light through the windows. If he didn't rest and warm up, he knew he'd die in the woods. A bitter wind clawed at his face.

To his delight the fireplace in the barn was still smoldering. Around it he spread his clothing, and then closed the double door behind him. A few small pieces of wood he added to the embers. In a minute the fire sprung to life. He added more wood. Heat radiated from the fire, wringing water from his clothing, warming his body, lifting his spirits. Despite his hunger, despite his depression, sleep rushed in. His back propped against the side of the hearth, his boots appeared to be steaming as his eyes closed.

Dreams flitted in and out of Joe's mind. In some ways they were coherent and others not, the meanings sometimes obscured. Early in his sleep cycle, he remembered standing by the apple tree talking with the other battalion commander and his exec. Unconsciously Joe grabbed a low lying limb, and then *BLAM!* A 20mm shell exploded in the tree; the two majors fell to the ground, entrails spilling from their abdomens. Joe looked into their eyes but they were not focusing, their gaze distant. One was dead; the other in shock would die within the half hour.

Deeper into the sleep his subconscious released things that

he would only understand years later, when the war was over and he was no longer in danger. Bats swooped low overhead. Shrill was their scream. First a few and then many came, darting, squealing, circling aimlessly.

Out of the swirling bats, a young man in army uniform appeared, sneering and peering at Joe from a sideward posture. His shoes wore a glassy polish, his uniform tailored to a fit, and he sported a Sam Browne belt. A visor peak officer's hat hid his eyes in the shadow, "You don't have what it takes, Joe Puett."

Joe stood up to him, "By God, we'll see about that." Face to face the two challenged each other, their war faces grimly set. An argument ensued. Each railing the other over passed failures and inadequacies. The dream faded.

OOO

A gray sky greeted a freezing morning. Somewhere a rooster crowed. For a minute Joe thought he was back home on the pulp-wood farm in Georgia. The fire was out and he was cold. More wood and a stoke or two and the fire flared. Joe smiled as the flames leapt up. He rubbed his hands together. About then, his stomach reminded him, he had not eaten in four days. In a grain crib, he found a mix of oats and wheat. It wasn't Cheerios and Wheaties, but mixed with water, it was edible. Boiled with water, it was tasty. Joe thanked God for breakfast, and then filled one overcoat pocket with the uncooked grain.

His movement south towards the friendly lines had its down side. The lines were constantly changing as German forces infiltrated the thinly dispersed American lines. A small group of American infantrymen attached themselves to Joe Puett, but to no avail. They ran into a German company on the edge of an evergreen forest. "Hands high," yelled the man with a Schmiesser machine pistol, his finger already on the trigger.

"The second *worst day of my life*," thought Joe Puett. His rag tag group dropped the few rifles and ammo bandoliers, then felt the depression setting in like the poison it is.

For Sgt. Bill Heinz, it was his first POW experience, for Joe Puett it was his second. They both were already plotting their escape. A more efficient group of guards processed them through, it wouldn't be easy. Interrogators seated at crude wooden tables asked questions, logged them into a bound book by name, rank and serial number. A secondary table, manned by a Wehrmach major was filtering out Jewish American soldiers.

The German major was somehow familiar. Joe studied his face and mannerisms, while trying to hide his own. Slowly, it came to him- Eugene Martz, the tire company representative in Atlanta. "No, no, not Martz, it was Mertz. Eugene Mertz. I'm sure of it. He thought to himself, "That son of a bitch is setting aside the Jewish guys."

Joe Puett was certain he would attempt another escape. Frantically, he searched for Sgt. Heinz in the crowded compound. "We've got to get out tonight, Sarge. Something bad is going on here."

Heinz responded, "There's a hole in the fence over there, Colonel. As soon as it's dark, we better go before the Krauts close it. We've got another hour 'til dark."

OOO

Joe Puett's second escape was like the first, cold, uncomfortable, but a whole lot better morale on the other side of the wire. Their first night was spent without the barn and cozy fire, huddled in a culvert under a bridge. In the dark and uncertain forest, he and Sgt Heinz found a friendly unit two days later. As soon as possible he got on the telephone to Corps Headquarters. "The Krauts are separating Jews from the other prisoners. They're up to no good."

As soon as he could, Joe Puett signed an affidavit to that effect. The incident went into the recesses of his mind until

April, 1948. The Nuremberg Trials had whittled their way down the command of the Einsatzgruppen, when Eugene Mertz surfaced and so did Joe's affidavit. Although Mertz was not an SS death squad member, he aided and abetted them. Sentenced to seven years in prison, he was freed in 1951. As a convicted war criminal, Mertz was denied entry to the United States in 1953.

OOO

Less than one percent of POW's escape their captors. Joe Puett did it twice. No medals for surviving the rigors of being a prisoner were available in WWII, but a medal was introduced in 1985 under Public Law 99-145. Joe Puett could have worn one with an oak leaf cluster and two 'V' for valor for the escapes. Contributing to the conviction of a war criminal was equally noteworthy. In army lingo, Joe Puett was a tough nut.

Four weeks after he saw his two fellow officers killed near the apple tree, a tiny fleck of metal surfaced on the side of his finger, the only part of the cannon shell that struck him.

If any sense could be made of a dream without psychoanalysis, Joe found his bats as the many details of commanding in combat, and his tormentor was himself. He indeed had what it took.

TWENTY ONE

JEDBURGH

In 1944 the Office of Strategic Services (OSS) sent 93 three man teams of specialists into France. Their objectives were to coordinate resistance efforts and to sabotage the German war effort. Two hundred and seventy-nine men and women would become known as Jedburghs. Several were Cajuns from Louisiana, whose French dialect was like Seventeenth Century, long forgotten in France.

Merlin Loiselle looked up from under the hood of his aging Peugeot. He was frustrated, steam rising from the radiator, the engine knocking from poor gasoline, apprehension boiling in his guts. The motorcycle coming towards him sputtered, its driver dressed in grey and topped with the familiar German helmet. With broken French interspersed with German, the soldier asked if he could help.

Merlin waved him off, shaking his head all the while. "No, no, it will be all right in a minute. It needs to cool down." As he threw the ignition switch, the engine and the knocking stopped.

The soldier was persistent. As he poured the contents of his canteen onto the engine block, still more steam rose from the hood. "Gut, es ist gut." He exclaimed as he remounted the cycle. Pulling his goggles down, he revved the engine and sped away.

Merlin wiped his forehead with a white handkerchief, a subtle but very meaningful signal.

Fifty meters up the road, the cyclist suddenly left his bike. A wire stretched across the narrow road went *twanggg* as he did. While the driver tumbled uncontrollably, two men emerged quickly from the underbrush. A pistol cracked once and then again. The soldier left the road by his heels, dragged to the cover of the underbrush. The motorcycle, now silent, followed him.

Merlin climbed back into the car, making sure he wasn't seen. He had no knowledge of the importance of the cyclist or the message he carried, if any. All he knew for sure was he was dead, the first war fatality Merlin had witnessed.

Cool spring air blew through the car and more importantly over the engine. He drove cautiously, driving an automobile he wouldn't have in peacetime, running late, the dreaded Gestapo everywhere. To wit, he'd aided the Maquis in killing a German soldier.

On the seat next to him, the map to Angers flapped nervously in the wind. Glancing periodically, Merlin watched for his turns, then rolled into town, past the massive 13th Century fortification. At the Romanesque and Gothic Cathedral of Angers, the Cathedral of St. Maurice, he stopped near a rear entrance. A priest greeted him and quickly led him to a room in the crypt. On the floor above, mass was just beginning, a choir's hymn resonated in the massive nave. "Gregorian chant," thought Merlin.

Five other men and one woman introduced themselves, first names only. The woman, Lucille, began, "We have a major supply drop coming in two days. We must get these supplies from the drop zone and to the users quickly, before the Bosch know it's happened. Right now they are doing everything to stop the invasion at Normandy. The drop will be in broad daylight. Each of you will have a hot color. The containers will be marked with your color and you and your people will take only your colored containers. They are designed to take six men to handle and three average automobiles or two small trucks to carry away the contents."

For a solid hour she briefed the gathering of Maquis, communists and Jedburghs. Abruptly, she dismissed them, "Mass is over. Vive la France."

As Merlin approached his car, he gazed up at the magnificent structure, its fabulous stained glass and lofty spires. The choir, still singing, expanded the dimension of godliness in a time of ungodliness. "Someday I'll come back as a tourist and see all of this. Magnificent."

The old engine whirred once, twice and then finally turned over, smoke blowing out the exhaust, back firing twice. Merlin winced at the noise and what it might attract. A gendarme passed him, his arms flailing away at the smoke, and faking a cough.

The supply drop would come in an open field near Tours. Merlin thought, "Wouldn't it be strange if it fell on the old battlefield where Charles Martel defeated the Umayyad Caliphate in A.D. 732?" His love of history undiminished by the war, he shook off the daydream.

OOO

Merlin crouched in the hedgerow, as four B-17's roared overhead at 1500 ft. He had expected transports, C-47's. From the bomb bays spilled a load of cylinders, olive drab with colored bands. Parachutes blossomed behind them, yanking the cylinders into a nose down attitude.

Men poured from the hedgerows from every direction. Two men seized each cylinder after disconnecting the parachute. In minutes the cylinders were gone. Engines of several vehicles cranked on the other side of the hedgerows and hastily left the scene.

A group of women appeared in single file from a corner of the field. Slowly they gathered the parachutes. Scissor blades flashed in the sunlight as they cut the chutes into large rectangles and neatly folded the material. The nylon chords they cut into three meter lengths. In mere minutes the women disappeared from the field, the parachutes, now only fabric, gone with them.

At the far end, a horse drawn mower began cutting. The shiny green stalks folded to the ground, severed from their roots to become hay. Any evidence of the trampling by the partisans was gone as the whirling blades did their work. Even as the field was returned to normal, the cylinders were being opened, their contents discharged. Sten guns, ammunition, hand grenades, explosives, medical supplies, radios and Spam flowed like manna from heaven. Well, maybe not the Spam.

The cylinders themselves disappeared in a variety of ways, beneath manure piles, buried directly in mother earth, cut up for scrap or, as half cylinders, became animal watering troughs.

For the first time since he arrived in France, Merlin had a firearm. The slow firing Sten gun slung over his shoulder, his passive resistance now active. He thought of the motor cycle courier, that was just the beginning. He shouldn't think of him with such remorse, after all, he was the enemy. But he did.

OOO

The not so trusty Peugeot rumbled along the dirt country road throwing a beige dust cloud, in the front seat next to him a member of the Maquis. Merlin knew him only as Rene. Last names were not important, even better not known.

Rene looked like the Maquis poster boy, twenty something, swarthy, a thin black mustache, black hair dipped beneath a black beret, a red bandana tied around his neck.

150

"Stop here," Rene demanded as they approached a side alley on the edge of town.

Merlin applied the brakes and looked ahead, checked the rear view mirror. Two more men appeared from nowhere, got into the car. They appeared grim, no salutations were exchanged. Rene signaled with an index finger to continue. "Turn right here. Turn left here. Right at this next street. Stop here. Wait for us." All three left the car and disappeared around the corner. Merlin waited, checked his watch. Three explosions rocked the quiet afternoon, followed by gunfire. The clearly familiar sounds of Sten guns, *dut-dut-dut-dut, dut-dut-dut.* Two more grenades, almost simultaneously, exploded.

The three partisans tumbled back into the car, "Go, go, go," shouted Rene. Merlin floored the gas peddle, the Peugeot hesitated, sprang to life just as a bullet penetrated the rear windshield. Small pieces of glass sprayed the interior of the car striking Merlin in the neck, Rene in the shoulder.

Merlin retraced his route, discharging his passengers, continuing to a side road in the country. With a tire iron, he broke out the corner of the window where the bullet left a tell-tale hole. Carefully, he extended the tear in the cloth head liner so it no longer looked like a bullet hole.

Rene had left him with only the sketchiest action report, "We killed about seven of them, but did not see the boss. The Gestapo is always varying their routines because of us. We hurt them all right, but not a big success. We must do better when we pull these things." Merlin could only give HQ a similar sketchy report with the next radio transmission.

OOO

In the back room of the farm villa, Merlin's radio operator, Marcel, tapped out his report in coded Morse code. Allied forces were only twenty or thirty kilometers away but German resistance had stiffened around St.Lo. He knew the expected longevity of spies in France, and he now in his fourth month.

Marcel finished, looked at his watch,"Thirty seconds under the maximum."

"Good, good, now destroy the paper notes," Merlin replied. The tiny room illuminated as the paper burned atop a dinner plate. The orange glow dimmed quickly, leaving only the light of the single candle and a puff of smoke. It was bed time.

OOO

Merlin rose from the crude wooden framed bed. Splashed water on his face but didn't shave. It was only then did he realize he had not put the car in the barn. Things were so hectic. He dressed quickly and grabbed the car keys as he threw open the door.

The car with the broken window worried Merlin, but with what was going on just a short distance away, there was no way to replace it. With the car door still open, he turned the key. A flash of light and searing heat enveloped Merlin. The blast threw him from the car onto the ground. He rolled trying to snuff the flames, pain reaching every part of his body, until at last his brain said "No more," and he slid into unconsciousness.

Marcel rushed to his side in seconds, pouring water on his face and head. Merlin's hair was gone, eyes staring mindlessly into the morning sky, face blackened like a minstrel. Marcel cradled him in his arms, rocking him like a child until he too was blinded by the tidal rush of his own tears.

OOO

June 6, 1994, Normandy, D-Day Celebration

A long day of speeches and memories filled the 50th anniversary of D-Day. In the crowd of thousands, a lone member of the 101st Airborne Division proudly displayed his Screamin' Eagles patch on a powder blue wind-breaker.

Merlin Loiselle commented, "I see you were with the 101st, did you see much action?"

The graying veteran snapped to attention, "Yessir. I saw it all, wounded twice I was in the first wave. I landed two miles from Ste. Mere Eglise with the 501st Regiment. You could say, I was one of the first Americans to invade Europe."

Merlin smiled with a smile that stretched the many facial scars, "I thank you for your service, my friend, but you are mistaken about being here first. I was here three months before you with the OSS. Just like you, I parachuted into France, but I was only wounded once." With that he turned ever so gently to expose the remnants of his ear, now just a mass of irregular scar tissue.

The two men embraced as long lost friends, not trying to hide their tears, their shoulders shaking in a common grief. They were both Americans on a patriotic day, where emotions lay exposed everywhere they looked.

Together they visited the American Cemetery at Collville sur Mer- and more tears. As they walked the cemetery they discovered that they both were from Louisiana, one from Lafayette, the other Lake Charles. They had a lot to talk about. Coonasses usually do.

OOO

June 8, 1994

Few Americans visit the cemetery at La Cambe because it isn't American, it's German. Merlin Loiselle did not really know why he found himself there. Yes, he could admit that the motor cycle courier seemingly died for no other reason than that he was German. He held no remorse for the Gestapo agents he helped kill. The courier was different.

Alone he walked the beautiful site where even the trees are numbered, graves meticulously kept, a large black cross looming in the background atop a grassy mound. In his left hand a small bouquet of flowers, "How could I possibly know which one out of so many?"

Row after row he read the names and ranks, the unit they were with, birth and death dates. In the midst of many, Merlin found one, Helmut Dengler. "Why not he?" he asked himself.

Bending down, and reverently, Merlin placed the bouquet on the grave. "I saw no malice in you. You even tried to help me. Maybe some day I will understand."

In the entry arch, Merlin read from the dedication plaque, *"..it is a graveyard for soldiers, all of whom had not chosen either the cause or the fight."* He found affirmation there.

TWENTY TWO

HERO OF A DIFFERENT STRIPE

November, 1942, Augusta, Georgia

He was tall and rather thin, with a noticeable limp, his black hair combed straight back. John Bond was military age, but the limp revealed an earlier battle with polio, and so he was 4-F, unfit for military duty.

The day was clear but cool, the house on 10th Street a typical two story crowded by its neighbors. John took a deep breath, grabbing the hand rail, mounting the four steps awkwardly, a yellow envelope grasped tightly in his right hand.

The doorbell buzzed, he waited, buzzed again. Edna Holmes opened the squeaky front door, "Yes, can I help you?"

John looked down at a slightly stout woman in her early fifties, graying hair and bifocals. Her head tipped back slightly to accommodate the lower lenses of the glasses.

"Mam, I have a telegram for Mrs. Edna Holmes. Are you Mrs. Holmes?"

Edna wiped her hands on a red and white apron, "Yes, I am." Her hand trembled as she reached out to take the yellow envelope. Only then did she see the black border on it. "Is it a death notice?" she asked.

"Yes, Mam, I'm afraid it is. Is there a friend or relative you'd like me to call?'

"No, I can't think … Is it Jimmy?"

"Mam, I haven't read the telegram, you'll have to open it."

The envelope vibrated with her trembling fingers as Edna tore it open. Again her head tilted back to read. Her lips moved but the words didn't come out, only mutterings.

"My boy is dead. Oh God, my boy is dead." Edna's legs weakened, and she began to fall.

Quickly John held her arm supporting the grief stricken woman. Tears welled behind the glasses, her face pale.

John repeated his question, "Is there someone I can call to help you, a friend or a relative?"

"My sister, call my sister. She responded. "Alice Wickham, her number is on the cover of the phone book."

John was already passed his official duty as delivery man, and into the process of compassion. He could never turn back. After coaxing the grieving mother to her easy chair, he called the sister from a hallway telephone. She arrived in minutes, already weeping bitterly.

Quietly, John removed himself from the scene. Mounted the wobbly bicycle and pedaled his way home. From the recesses of his subconscious, he remembered the photograph of a marine on the table next to the easy chair. Jimmy Holmes, USMC, was dead, his widowed mother childless. There would be no funeral in three days, no gathering of friends and relatives. This was war time, and Jimmy Holmes was already buried on a stinking island in the Pacific. With the sleeves of his woolen jacket, John wiped the tears from his cheeks. He felt a growing constriction in his throat. "Damn this war, damn it," the heat rising inside of him.

Three days later, John pedaled his way back to 10th Street, a florist's bouquet of flowers in his hand. He pressed the buzzer, and soon Edna Holmes answered. "Oh, it's you the man from Western Union."

"Yes, Mam, my name is John Bond. I just wanted you to know I was thinking of you." He held out the bouquet.

"How lovely." She exclaimed. Her eyes were red, she looked as pale as the day the telegram arrived, and John felt helplessness creeping in. "I'll stop by in a couple days to see how you're doing."

As he picked up the bicycle, John noticed the little flag in the window, a red border, and a gold star on a white field. It would not be the last such flag he would see in Augusta. Twenty-seven times, John climbed the front stairs of houses with people inside, and brought them the awful news. Twenty-seven times a little bit of him died. "Somebody had to do it, he said years later. "They never had an officer or a chaplain to bring them the bad news, just me. I never got use to it."

Heroes come in many forms, not all are in uniform.

TWENTY THREE

TEARS FOR THE RED
AND THE WHITE

For two months, Flying Officer Stanislaus Kubayacz evaded Nazis while trying desperately to get to England. For two more months he trained in RAF Squadron 303, patiently waiting his chance to fight again. Then, on a routine training mission off the Scottish Coast came a radio message that changed it all, "Nazis, eleven o'clock low."

July, 1940

Stash was shocked at what he saw, a flight of twenty-seven Heinkle 111's and no escorting fighters. The British squadron commander slowly turned the formation of Hawker Hurricanes. He issued his orders calmly, the sun riding above his left shoulder, the oxygen regulator blinking faster, the enemy bombers maintaining their formation as if unopposed. Eleven Poles followed, spoiling for a fight.

"Red-one to Cowslip, we have twenty-seven bandits, fifty

159

miles south-east of Montrose. We are attacking, now."

OOO

At Fighter Command HQ, puzzled faces showed everywhere. "What the devil is Red Squadron doing up there?' "Isn't that the Polish Squadron?" "Get them out of there."

It was far too late; emotions far too strained to hold them back. Red-one dove at the Heinkles. Eight machine guns chattered in unison, the tracers already sewing a seam across the left engine of the lead German aircraft.

The formation broke as the leader faded to the left, trailing a long black line of oily smoke. Parachutes blossomed, billowing white against the sky, three, four, five of them.

Stash realized it was his turn as his element leader banked, turned and dove. Stash followed as he kicked rudder to gain some spacing. Looking at his slip indicator he was satisfied, when he looked up the enemy plane filled his gun sight. The guns shook, tracers flying, the smell of cordite filling the cockpit, the full thunder of the eight chewing apart his target.

Stash barely missed flying into the bomber, it all happened so quickly. Looking over his shoulder, he could see flaming debris everywhere, the main body of the bomber in a near vertical attitude. He pulled up, his vision tunneling, hyper ventilating, his heart pounding. "Red Squadron, regroup," crackled the radio.

By then the German bombers had scattered, and Red-one issued orders to each pair of fighters. Stash followed his element leader after a lone Heinkle headed north-east. Catching up easily, they attacked as before. This time he was prepared for the timing, his gunsight filled with the enemy's silhouette. His shot train was tearing into the right engine as the other Hurricane worked on the left one. The bomber simply exploded.

In the distance, Stash could see another bomber getting

away, but fuel was too low to give chase. The victory of the moment was thrilling. They headed back to base, the green grass field a welcomed sight at last. He thought of Poland. He was bursting with emotion and pride, but he wanted to cry. Most of all, he wanted to cry for Poland.

His engine whined to a stop, the tears didn't.

OOO

A month later, August 13

A bell clanged repeatedly. Twelve pilots rushed to their Hurricanes, strapping parachutes, buckling harnesses, the engines already idling. In groups of four they thundered down the grassy field, bouncing on the edge of airborne. Then, majestically, they rose as one into a cloudless sky.

In minutes they joined a larger group that stretched for a mile or so. Stash had never seen so many friendly aircraft in one formation. Almost giddy, he pulled his four ship flight into position. Ahead in the blue of a clear afternoon, he could see the Hun, black dots, hundreds of them, bombers with fighter escorts.

Climbing, climbing to gain speed in the dive, turning, turning to gain position with the sun, the giant wing proceeded. The radios remained silent for all this time, and then the silence broken, "Blue leader to blue wing, attacking now." In graceful peeling, the Hurricanes winged over, curved gracefully downward.

Stash smiled beneath his mask, "How terribly British. So calm and collected was Blue-leader." His turn to peel-off soon came, with precision stick and rudder, his engine surging, gun switches in the 'on' position. His head cleared of the g-forces, hurtling at a Heinkle's ten o'clock, the silhouette filling his gun sight lens. *Daka, daka, daka,* rattled the eight guns. The stream of tracers arced into the bomber's cockpit as Stash passed through the splintering formation. As he pulled up to gain altitude, two Bf-109's passed from left to right. He kicked right rudder, pushed the stick hard to the right, and held the trigger. The long arc of shells ran across both aircraft, from tail to nose as he eased up on the stick. Both rolled slowly, one left and one right until they collided in a fire ball.

Into a diving turn he went to clear his tail. Nothing there, not even his wing man who was lost within seconds of the attack on the Heinkle. Dodging, turning, his own tail to cover in the melee, the wing man had simply disappeared.

For four years, Flying Officer Kubayacz had trained for this moment, and the moment took exactly forty-nine seconds to accomplish. For the remainder of the sortie, he, like his inexperienced wing man, dodged enemy fighters, occasionally sending a spurt from his guns, but never connecting. This had been Goering's "Adler Tag," or "Eagle Day," and it was not his victory to claim.

Stash would fly one hundred and thirteen sorties in all during the war but never again shoot down an enemy plane. Escorting bombers, and then attacking targets of opportunity on his return, he filled his log book. His personal record of victories ended at four and a half. He would remember with pride those victories long after the war, and only a little regret that he was not an ace.

OOO

At the 1994 D-Day Celebration, an aging Stanislaus Kubayacz was interviewed by an American author. "I was one of the *Few*, who won the Battle of Britain. It's a shame that Churchill didn't remember that when he went to Yalta. One hundred forty-five Poles fought in it, more than Canada, more than New Zealand. Only seven Americans took part. Thirty of my country men died in that battle, but we shot down one hundred and twenty-six of the enemy. The Brits made a movie of the battle. I was disappointed. They depicted us as a bunch of undisciplined chatter boxes. Nothing could be further from the truth. I was there. I know how the Poles fought. Because we got close to the targets, they said we were reckless. At six hundred yards, the Brits couldn't hit the ocean, and neither could we. We got close. We got results."

Stash Kubayacz smiled, patting his breast, "I love my Poland." A red and white enameled pin graced the lapel of his English tweed. "I love my Poland. He repeated, "But I never could go back," and again, unaltered by time, the tears for Poland.

TWENTY FOUR

DOWN BY HIS BOOT STRAPS

February 1944, over Germany

The bomb run went well. Four tons of 250 lb. bombs left the bomb bay, well almost four tons. The bomb bay doors failed to close, a single bomb had hung up between the door and the side of the bomb bay opening. The drag would soon leave the B-24 behind the formation, and fighters would find them alone and nearly defenseless.

Sgt. Bob Dufries heard the commotion over the intercom and crept his way through the passageway forward to the bomb bay. His tail gunner position now unmanned, his problem solving abilities and his courage were about to be tested.

Three gunners and the bombardier had gathered around the windy opening when Bob arrived. The bombardier volunteered, "It's not armed yet. The arming wire is gone, but the arming vane is still there. That's the little propeller on the nose." They were at twelve thousand feet and a blast of cold air was rushing through the opening. Bob took one look around. It was clear he was the smallest of the five.

"Hand me that fire extinguisher," he shouted above the wind. He quickly decided who the sturdiest two were. "You two grab my ankles and hold me while I loosen this thing."

While Bob dangled out over space, he felt the rush of freezing air intensify. Awkwardly he banged the extinguisher against the bomb, *clang, clang, clang*. The bombardier winced, but the bomb didn't move an inch. "Pull me up, Bob shouted.

"We need something to pry it with."

The bombardier presented the crank for manually lowering the landing gear in the event of hydraulic failure. "Like this?" He asked.

"Yeah, that's good," Bob responded. By the ankles again he dangled over space. As he pried on the reluctant ordinance, he suddenly realized that his parachute was back at his gun position. Below he could see a winter clad Germany, rivers, towns and a few scattered clouds. He felt his strength wilting as the cold air rushed over him. The prying motion suddenly began having some effect on the reluctant bomb. "One more time," he said to himself, but it didn't budge. At the end of his endurance, "Now damn it," he blurted.

Miraculously, the bomb let loose. Immediately, the arming vane started turning like a pinwheel. Bob watched it go, as he dangled by his ankles over the abyss of twelve thousand feet. The bomb with the yellow rings around its nose headed for terra firma. Bob came up feet first to the floor of the bomber. He wanted to lie there a moment, nausea and dizziness were creeping in. "Good job," said the bombardier. The gunners said nothing, patting him gently on the shoulders. The bomb bay doors whirred closed. The rush of wind stopped.

Bob placed the crank back into its rightful place, "I better get back to my gun." As he passed the waist gun positions, "My parachute is back there too." The gunners laughed. Just then, the intercom squawked, "We're still above ten thousand feet, everybody on oxygen,"

The superchargers whirred as the full power of the four engines regained the safety of the formation. Bob Dufries cleared the bolt on his .50 caliber, strapped on his parachute, and latched the buckles. "What a way to earn a living," as he buckled his mask. The nausea and the dizziness faded as the flood of oxygen reached his brain.

OOO

News of Bob's space walk traveled through the Fifth Air Force all the way to the top. Hap Arnold heard about it a few days later and decided, "That man deserves a Bronze Star." Who would object? Thirty days later, at a group ceremony, Bob Dufries received the Bronze Star.

In 2001 he showed the award to a friend, "I didn't think it was that big a' deal."

His friend suggested, "I guess the bomb hit a Catholic elementary school in France?"

Bob laughed, "No, I think it hit a defense plant in Germany. Yeah, yeah, that's it, a critical defense plant in Germany. It was making rocket engines for the V-2."

The truth is, nobody but God knows what happened to the troublesome bomb.

OOO

Bob Dufries never completed his thirty-five missions. Plagued with chronic nose bleeds that forced his crew to abort their mission, he was grounded. In his new job, he was able to tell authorities where nearly forty unexploded bombs were located. Using Fifth Air Force aerial photos and transparent overlays, he could pinpoint their locations. The German UXB forces were able to locate and defuse them after the war was over, and before new construction begun.

167

In all candor he would say, "Bombs are always a problem for somebody."

TWENTY FIVE

SILENT RUNNING

German u-boats by the score litter the oceans' bottom floor
Endless pinging no longer heard thru sealed compartment door.
"Alarm, alarm," they hear no more, ghostly crews lie unperturbed,
Their rusting metal coffins stay motionless, soundless,
*   undisturbed.*

U-nine-eight-one and three-oh-nine the list is long indeed,
Their glory days are over now, no bells and horns to heed.
No training dives or depth charges to make one's senses leave.
No rotting food or other smell to make one gag and heave.

So solemnly, silently, the wake of ocean's claim
No more ribbons for your chest, no more fleeting fame.
Die Kriegsmarine is quieted, no more songs to sing
'Til judgment day rolls around and souls to judgment wing.

P repare to surface." bellowed the intercom. Peter Glotzbach, relieved at last from the depth charge attack, wiped his brow with a dirty rag. His balance wavered a bit when he came to his feet. The odors of the boat worsened as the sub extended its dive duration, and that had been a long one.

Air rushed in from the open hatches on the conning tower and over the crews' quarters. The odors vanished in minutes, all but the diesel fuel, the source of which sloshed beneath the floor grate with an equal amount of seawater. Rotten food, body odors, farts, battery acid, all whisked out the hatches. He took a deep breath of the sea air.

His beard was four weeks old, his color pale, his hair gone shaggy, but his hopes were high. Peter thought the patrol would soon end and maybe it would be his last. Hamburg was only hours away. Ah, Hamburg and beer, girls, sauerbraten, fresh sausage, girls. He was single and barely twenty. Five war patrols were enough for anyone, but would the Admiralty agree, that was the question.

The diesels chugged, wide open, as U-982 made its dash through the gray zone of Allied and German air control. The batteries were not fully charged when a dot appeared on the horizon astern. "Alarm, alarm, aircraft two-seven-oh," cried the lookout. Scrambling feet ran the ladders, "Battle stations, battle stations, emergency dive," barked the captain. Horns blared. A rush of water filled the ballast tanks.

Above, a British Typhoon cut loose its cannons. *Thump, thump, thump, thump,* the shells struck the deck behind the conning tower. Seconds later, water was pouring into the sleeping quarters. "Abort the dive, abort the dive, shouted the captain. "Lookouts to the bridge," again feet clattered on the ladders. The Typhoon was gone, or perhaps just beyond the clouds. The lookouts strained to spot it, binoculars glued to their foreheads.

A splash of seawater greeted him, as Peter raised the aft hatch to assess the damage. He was horrified at what he saw, oval holes twenty centimeters long and nearly as wide. Repairs would take hours. Damage control was the main reason he was in the crew, and now he had to perform his duty in a rolling sea with enemy aircraft lurking about.

Although the captain quickly called for air cover, none was promised. He looked helplessly at the huge holes; even from the tower they looked menacing. It was evident that they needed the ability to dive; Allied aircraft and surface vessels were still a threat.

Peter approached the conning tower, "Sir, I have an idea."

The captain motioned for him to come up, his white cap the only visible sign of his authority. A half eaten pencil rolled from one side of his mouth to the other, "Tell me your idea, Glotzbach."

"Sir, this boat has a double hull, if we cut a piece out of the outer hull and weld it over the damaged area, we should be able to dive to twenty meters or so."

"How long, Glotzbach?" asked the captain.

"I guess two hours, but can't guarantee it."

The captain spit out the pencil, "Get started. I hope you can do this in a rain squall because that's where we are headed."

Peter looked over the bow, an ominous cloud hung over the ocean, rain spewing out of it in a torrent. Waves sloshed across the deck, foamy white as they broke.

Two machinist mates, Kerr and Vogel, wrestled with the oxyacetylene tanks, hoses and torch. Tops of icy waves splashed over them as they did. In minutes, Peter was cutting away at a section of the after deck, a mask protecting his face and eyes, the splashing water slowing his progress, doubt beginning to creep into his mind.

With the first of his two hours quickly gone, the rain lessened. In mere minutes they would clear the protection of the rain squall. As the piece of outer hull came lose, Peter removed his mask to examine the inner hull. He could see no damage from his cutting.

Except for a few jagged edges the holes were flat. The torch cut threw the edges like a hot knife on butter. The three men strained with the large piece of steel as they positioned it over the cannon damage. A wave slapped at the group, only their static lines holding them to the deck. Cold water surged over their collars, soaking their necks, chilling their bones.

They wrestled the awkward steel plate into place. Two mates held it still while Peter began welding, the rod turning white hot, metal flowing like molasses onto the edge of the patch. Completing first the two ends with their narrow dimension, Peter then repositioned himself to do the long dimensions. Steam rose from the welds. "Was the seawater cooling the weld too fast?" He wondered.

The rain stopped, the boat clearing the rain squall, heading east. Sunlight spilled through the overcast as the boat knifed through two meter waves towards Hamburg, and home. The welding continued, the lookouts nervously watching the sky and the horizon, expecting to see land at any minute.

OOO

Coastal Command, London

Lt. Jeffrey Fellans carried the communiqué to the district office commander, Captain Quigly. "Sir, we have a u-boat on the ropes outside the Hamburg estuary. It's been hit by one of our typhoon aircraft, but dove away from the attack. The pilot claimed several hits and the boat must be unable to stay submerged. We need a destroyer or frigate to cut her off."

Captain Quigly looked at the wall map behind him, "HMS Furness is in position to give chase, radio her at once."

"Yes sir, Furness it is." The lieutenant disappeared down the hallway to ops ready room and the radio.

OOO

Peter Glotzbach was just finishing his last stretch of weld, when the lookouts yelled, "Alarm, alarm, ship bearing two-six-zero degrees and closing." The lookouts scampered below, the horns blew. As Peter pushed the acetylene gear over board, the hoses wrapped Vogel's leg. His static line just removed, Vogel slid off the deck and over the bulging hull of the boat. Peter desperately grasped at the welding apparatus, but managed only to grab the torch. Heat and pain shot through his hand to his brain. Reflexes told him to let go, but he could not. Vogel's eyes filled with terror as he dangled against the side of the hull.

In an instant, Vogel was thrown by a frothy whitecap back onto the deck, the hoses still entangling his leg. Kerr strained against the weight of the tanks to rid Vogel of the hoses. At last the whole mess of it turned loose. With clanging reminiscent of a harbor buoy, it disappeared into the sea. Kerr quickly hooked his mate's static harness to his own.

Clutching his burned hand, Peter headed for the aft hatch, behind him the two mates came panting. Once to the hatch, Kerr detached the static line. Wet hands slipped from the ladder, and they tumbled out of control. The three of them hit the floor as one, knees into chins, shoes into faces and one shoe into one groin. Above, a seaman closed the hatch, the dive bell still ringing in their ears. Moaning followed the clanging bell, but they could not move from the floor. The smell of diesel fuel soon became the taste of diesel fuel, as the boat nosed down for the dive angle. The stinky fuel mixed with seawater squirted through the floor grate into their gasping mouths. In unison, they spat.

Peter looked up from the floor, "Twenty meters, no more." He stared at the location of the patch just meters away. "Twenty meters," he repeated. He felt the boat turning hard right, south, away from Hamburg.

He came to a sitting position on the floor as did the two mates. The destroyer was pinging, getting closer. "I don't know if I can take this again," he mumbled.

The intercom squawked,"Rig for silent running."

Peter switched off the vent fans, the bilge pumps, even the nearly empty food locker. From a bunk, he lifted a pail full of tools and placed it on the floor as a precaution. The mates slipped into their bunks, realizing that the skinny mattresses had been soaked with sea water and riddled with shrapnel. There was nothing more they could do but pray. The sub leveled off, but Peter could not judge the depth. The sound of the sub's single screw was minimal, probably doing three or four knots.

Through the silence, a creaking sound came from the patch, Peter held his breath. The creaking stopped. "It's still hot," he whispered.

Swoosh, swoosh, swoosh went HMS Furness as it passed astern of the sub. The pinging had ceased. No depth charges were being dumped, a good sign. "The destroyer is getting some false signals on their sonar," thought Peter. He looked up at the four cannon shell holes, the patch continuing to hold, his flash light beam trembling.

OOO

U-982 cruised quietly down the Elbe, entering the harbor, turning sharply into the concrete bunker. Nobody lifted a head to see it glide through the still waters. On the river banks, the rumble of the diesels was silenced by the gusting winds. An unspectacular sunset painted the boat's return, gray, beneath a layer of gray, like black and white film in the camera. In the Glory Days, they would have a band, girls with floral bouquets, even Admiral Doenitz to hand out awards, but times were different. A u-boat a day was being lost at sea. The Allies had solved the submarine menace; hearsay said the enemy had an acoustical homing torpedo. The Ardennes offensive had stalled in the west and the Red Army advancing in the east. All of the news was bad and U-982 had no ships to report sunk, not a one. Their precious torpedoes still snuggly fit in the hold.

The celebration, one of survival rather than victory, did not ring with laughter.

A low rumble of many conversations was punctuated with

outbursts of insobriety. Beer, wine, fresh sausage, crusty bread and potatoes were served, but no lobster. "Why, no lobster? We always had lobster." Peter wondered, but inside, he had his own answer. No nurses from the military hospital attended the affair, and Admiral Doenitz wasn't even mentioned. He had his answers to those too.

Schnapps had poured freely before the air raid sirens began, and the party, plus the schnapps stumbled down the many steps to the shelter. Within minutes the bombs rumbled, big, big blasts that shook the earth and the shelter. With his hand wrapped in gauze, Peter thought about the day's events and the patch. "We probably saved the boat and fifty five men with that patch. The destroyer thought they were getting false signals because we were so shallow." He managed a smile at the irony. "Where the hell is Doenitz?" With his good hand, he took another swig from the bottle, a long one at that.

In a clear tenor voice, Peter began to sing "Das U-Boot Lied," At once two others joined in, then two more and then a chorus, "Die Stunde hat geschlagen---.." Their song resonated in the great cavity of the shelter like the ghosts of a Wagnerian tragedy.

OOO

The patch had indeed saved fifty-five men of the U-982; the boat itself did not see action again. A Tall Boy bomb broke the concrete bunker above it and tore the top surface of the boat to pieces. The crew was indeed saved, and was never sent back to sea again. It made up a portion of the twenty-five percent that returned. The seventy-five percent who never returned made the Kriegsmarine the highest mortality rate of all World War II military units.

Peter Glotzbach worked as a machinist in Hamburg after the war. He received no medal for his hand in saving the boat and its crew. His hand never received any medical attention except his own. The only thanks came from Vogel in a quiet moment between the bombs and the u-boat songs.

TWENTY SIX

HORKI

December, 1942, Soviet Belarus

*His family farm was half way between Horki and Smolensk, but the other partisans called him "Horki." At fifteen years of age, Horki carried his own weight in the partisan effort. Nobody thought of him as an orphan taking up space and food in the company, but he **was** an orphan and the family farm lay in ruin a short distance from the Dnieper.*

Living in makeshift shelters and eating rations that would gag a buzzard, the lad became tougher still. Life on the farm was torturous, but this was worse by far, and death could come at any second. The hated Storches searched constantly for Horki and his comrades. The spindle legged aircraft flew slowly but could send fighter-bombers, a company or a regiment of Nazis at them with the click of a radio button.

The company commander was the crustiest Russian of a group of crusty Russians. His real name was Vladimir Malenovsky but to the men he was Vlad, "Vlad the Impaler" to some, "Uncle Vlad" only to

Horki. Vlad was nearly sixty, but hid his age well. Except for the white hair, he appeared much younger. Bushy eyebrows and smooth skin gave him the appearance of a Cossack. He clenched a small clay pipe between his teeth, but rarely smoked it. As a partisan he had the most necessary quality of being unpredictable.

Vlad's map was old, stained with three different color of mess, and torn at the folds. In the light of the kerosene, he studied it. "Horki, come here. What is the terrain like west of here for say ten kilometers?"

"Here is swamp, now frozen but maybe you break through the ice. Here is evergreen forest easy to travel. Here and here is sparse forest of birch tree and scrub low growth."

"Good, good, replied Vlad. Tonight we travel ten kilometers after dark and attack the airfield that sends the Storches."

Horki's eyes lit up, "Uncle Vlad, are we that close to the nest?"

Vlad smiled, "That's what the girls tell me."

Horki's lip curled up on the left, "Girls?"

"Yes, the two who came into camp this afternoon. They appear to be your age, but don't get any ideas. You can still get shot for liaisons with fellow partisans."

"I didn't see them come in, are they good looking?" Vlad pretended to be angry, "I said don't get any ideas. What difference does it make if they are good looking or if they look like Russian wolf hounds?" As he turned away from Horki, he was grinning. His gold tooth glistened in the glow of the lamp.

"Look here, at my sketch, the runway is unpaved and runs generally east and west. The Storches will be at the west end of the runway, which is why we must attack from the south west rather than from the east end. Also we get better cover from the forest at the west end. You, my friend must destroy the Storches. Korko will give you two grenades as soon as he finds some. Hopefully, we will keep the garrison busy long enough for you to work. Any questions?"

Horki shook his head but said nothing. It was an hour before dark and already he began preparing his clothing and equipment. The burp gun ammo drum was full from the last operation; his boots lined with rags, his wool cap a crimson red, his coat a Russian army issue with three remaining buttons. Carefully, he placed a lump of lard into a sardine can and rolled the lid closed. The can slid into the left pocket of his coat next to a sugar cube still wrapped in cellophane. "Dinner," thought Horki.

Into an inside pocket he placed a wire cutters, a pen knife, his compass and an American cigarette lighter, the pocket flap closed with a button hole, but that button was also gone.

A wide leather belt surrounded his skinny waist, and he pulled the buckle to the last available hole. To the belt he attached a canvas kit bag. "Grenades, I'll believe when I see. Korko is an idiot. We should trade him to the Germans for a case of canned meat," he thought.

Horki operated the bolt of the burp gun, filling the chamber, latching the safety, assuring himself he was ready. Outside he could hear the others assembling. Thoughts of his family came to mind, but only briefly. He opened the flimsy door and stepped into the cold. The front of the column had already trudged up the snow covered embankment headed west. Along the shuffling column, Horki searched for Korko and the promised grenades. But Korko was nowhere to be found.

OOO

Vlad waved his right arm; the squad leaders could barely see him in the dark and failed to see his signal. He cursed, lighting the flare, tossing it three or four meters into the air, hoping a sentry somewhere close didn't also see it.

Each squad had an objective, and painfully long seconds ticked as they positioned themselves. "Now dammit, now," Vlad said to himself, yet another interlude of time weighed on him, stretching his nerves. At last a volley of gunfire, grenades were exploding in the tents and corrugated metal buildings. He strained to see the silhouettes of aircraft at the west end. "Come on, Horki, do your business. We have little time."

OOO

Horki's kit bag was empty when he approached the Storches, no grenades. Four mechanics nervously stood by watching the fireworks at the camp a half mile away.

From the darkness, the fire of Horki's burp gun sent them tumbling into a bloody heap.

A drum of fuel sat adjacent to the first Storch. Horki quickly twisted the hose loose, and tipped it over. As he pulled one of the rags from his boot, a pool of gasoline washed under both of the aircraft. Dipping the end of the rag into the spilled fuel he backed up and lit it with his lighter.

The darkness erupted into bright yellow light as the fuel ignited. No longer shrouded in darkness, two other aircraft immerged. Twin engine Bf-110's sat fifty meters away on the opposite side of the field, their gray camouflaged frames sporting yellow engine nacelles. "Damn you, Korko. Where are my grenades?"

From the fires at the camp, Horki could see men running toward him. Time was running out. Racing to the 110's, he put a burst of shells into the engine hoping to start a fire. No fire erupted. Without success he tried the same tactic with the second 110. Desperate, he looked at the nose of the aircraft, "How can I disable this thing?"

Horki noticed the little metal tube protruding from the underside of the nose. It was metal and had a right angle bend. Taking careful aim, he shot it away, and then the second aircraft too. The farm boy had no idea what it was for. Trusting only his instincts, he shot them away.

He sprinted to the forest, bullets whizzing overhead, lungs

filling with the freezing night air, heart pounding, suddenly realizing that he was alone. The forest once reached was no guarantee. Germans could follow one man. He had no ambush set to cover him, and so he ran. The snow tugged against every stride, and he was tiring. How far he should travel south before turning east, he wondered. He should have thought about being chased, but it never came up for discussion to say nothing of being alone in a darkened forest.

Slowed also by his own lack of stamina, Horki stuck to the woods. Only the luminous dial of his compass kept his direction true. Vlad's dirty map passed through his memory, his own advice about the swamp now surfacing to his own welfare. He turned east.

For half an hour he traveled in that direction, frequently checking his compass. The temperature dropped so that every puddle turned to ice and crunched noisily beneath his boots. At last he stopped, propping himself against a birch tree, his gloved hand snug to the trigger guard. He rested.

In the still of the dark night, owls hooted, and screeched, the wind whipped through a hundred places that whistled. Convinced he was not followed, his march resumed at a slower pace.

The sun peaked over the steppes, but winter kept an icy grip. Horki rested again, fumbled for the sardine can. Cautiously, he opened the jagged edge and scooped a finger full of lard. It melted in his mouth like the creamiest butter, another and another until it was gone. The cube of sugar followed, melting on his tongue like Swiss chocolate. In minutes he felt the strength return to his body. He stood up, but his knees trembled, cold and weak. Worse yet, his feet were cold, the first warning of frost-bite.

An hour after sunup, he looked into a clear blue sky. No Storches circled above looking for partisans. The raid was a success, only what the cost? Horki knew it would not be all good news when at last he dragged himself into camp. His circuitous route had added at least three hours to his trip, but the plan had succeeded. With a compass check, and the position of the sun, he was sure he was close. He wondered if the Bf-110's were properly disabled, or would he see them flying around where the Storches couldn't, strafing anything that moved, any smoke column, or suspected redoubt. Soon he would have the answers, just over the next ridge, the one with the rusty looking rock outcrop.

Horki stopped in his tracks; up ahead an explosion rocked the stillness of the morning, followed by two other blasts. In the middle of a clearing, he found himself exposed. He dashed to the woods, expecting shots to follow, imagining bullets exiting his chest, spraying his red blood on the white snow. After diving headlong into cover, he was motionless. The snow packed against the side of his face melted sending little rivers of ice water down his neck, but he didn't move.

From the other side of the ridge, voices came. German, orders, shouted like on a parade ground, the Einsatzgruppen at work destroying the camp and anyone in it. An hour later, the Nazi killers left the scene. Horki cautiously entered the still smoldering camp.

The roofs of the huts were gone from the explosions; a smattering of crude furniture littered the ground, but no bodies. The company had escaped, or else never returned from the raid on the airfield. Vlad could have changed his plan and gone to a different camp or village. One thing was for sure, the company wasn't there, only Korko.

Korko was tied to a tree with baling wire; his eyes were plucked from his head and his body riddled with bullets. A hunting knife nailed a paper note to his chest. Horki didn't bother to read it. He'd seen them before. "Partisan: this will happen to you if…"

From behind a slight rise in the terrain, came voices, soft, Russian, casual. Horki released the safety on his weapon, and approached cautiously. The girls sat on a wool army blanket, smoking cigarettes, laughing, counting money.

Horki, moving slowly, stepped into view of the girls. Startled at first, they smiled. The older one, perhaps eighteen, spoke, "What are you doing here?"

The two looked like sisters, white straw-like hair, blue eyes, and like most Russians in wartime, overly thin. Their money in hand became nervous evidence and they awkwardly attempted to place it out of sight. In a nearby tree, a raven squawked ominously.

Horki leveled his weapon, "I might ask you the same question, but I have some others. For instance, are you whores or collaborators, or both?" He pulled the trigger.

The burp gun roared until the ammo ran out and the bolt popped open. Their blood splattered the snow drift behind them. The money, like Judas' silver, jumped into the air, looped like autumn leaves, then settled all around the blanket.

In the frozen earth, Horki dug a shallow grave for Korko. He asked God to accept his spirit even though Korko was an idiot. Marking the grave with a partly burned board, he scribed with a knife, "Korko- Partisan." The two girls he dragged to the clearing for the vultures and the wild dogs to find.

He checked his compass, shouldering his weapon, turning to the north-east, heading for a home that was no more – Horki.

OOO

In 1968, with the help of a ghost writer, Sergei Federov wrote his memoirs of fighting with the partisans, titled "Horki." Near the end of the writing, the ghost writer asked him if he ever thought about all of this. He replied, "The war ended twenty-three years ago, but I am reminded every day about something sinister, gruesome or downright revolting. I found out later that the things I shot off the two bombers were called pitot tubes. The tube controls the airspeed indicator. No pilot would fly without it"

The writer then asked, "Do you ever think of the two girls?"

"I try not to think of them, but they sometimes haunt my dreams."
"When was the last time that happened?"
Sergei smiled nervously. He took a deep breath, "Last night."

TWENTY SEVEN

THROUGH THE MIND OF A CHILD

Denny was only four years old when the Japs bombed Pearl Harbor. It was two years later before he was aware that America was at war. First grade nun, Sister Mary Raphael, sold war stamps that he glued into a yellow cardboard folder, ten cents each. Some day he'd trade the folder in for a war bond that would buy tanks and planes and stuff to fight the war- $18.75. Then later he'd get his money back plus $6.25, sounded like a good deal, especially when Mom supplied the dimes.

Once a month air raid sirens blared in the neighborhood. Dad donned a white WWI looking helmet and went down the street to his post- whatever that meant. At home all the lights went out and everybody sat in the living room. "Aren't we supposed to be in the basement?" One of the older brothers asked. Nobody replied, and we stayed in the living room where it was more comfortable than the scary basement. A place to be avoided, the basement was dark, damp and had shelves with empty jars and not much else. Boogey men were mentioned on a couple occasions, those never seen, never heard, always threatening ghosts of someone's imagination, certainly not Denny's.

In the North Park Theater he watched his second movie, "God Is My Copilot." It struck him odd that bad people would try to shoot down good American Flying Tigers. What were they thinking? They almost always lost, riddled to pieces by the good guys. "Blown to smithereens," was the phrase most used. Even then, Denny wondered how the bullets struck the Jap planes at ninety degrees rather than at an angle- like from behind. Oh well, that's Hollywood. Years later he would notice high altitude contrails in a cowboys and Indians movie. Can't fool that Denny.

At age seven, some facts about the movie stayed with him for the rest of his life, tucked back in the mental recesses for no good reason. Jap airplanes didn't have self-sealing gas tanks and so when hit by machine gun bullets, they exploded- *poof.* The Curtis Warhawk, the Flying Tigers flew, was called a P-40, and it couldn't out turn the Japanese fighters. It could out dive them though - good to know in a dog fight. Finally, the shark's mouth painted on the P-40 was to scare the Japs. Denny didn't believe that for a minute, but it was neat looking even if it didn't scare anyone. Oh, and the P-40 had self-sealing gas tanks, so when our guys got shot down, they had a chance to bail out. Denny liked that feature, no *poof.* Hit the silk, Scotty!

The main man in the story was Robert Scott played by actor Dennis Morgan. In 2002, a year after Denny's retirement, he bought the book "God Is My Copilot," and left it at the museum counter to be autographed by the author. A week later, the book arrived in the mail, "Signed especially for Denny Rath - Best wishes. Bob Scott." Heroes don't ever die, do they?

OOO

The first movie, a birthday deal Mom cooked up would be "Dumbo," the baby circus elephant. They went at night and

Mom got tired and tried to sell Denny the idea that he was tired. Bottom line- Denny only got to see half the movie. The only connection he could make between the first and the second movie was Dumbo and the Flying Tigers could both fly. Denny wanted to fly too, someday.

For the meantime, flying meant the dining room chair and a piece of broom handle for a stick and lots of *daka, daka, daka*. Sometimes demoting himself to a B-17 gunner, the same broom handle pointed out the window like a .50 caliber, and in his imagination, he fought the war. A game for him, but he knew deep inside, somewhere people were getting killed in numbers he could not yet comprehend.

OOO

On a clear autumn day, a real P-40 went out of control over Denny's neighborhood. His brothers pointed skyward, yelling excitedly. "He bailed out, the pilot bailed out." Denny never saw what all the fuss was about, but the brothers were right. Moments later, the P-40 crashed into a hangar at the Curtis-Wright plant killing a painter.

That evening Denny's grandfather died. Denny hardly knew him, so there was no burden of grief thrown on the six year old. He continued playing with the wax teeth and lips they sold at the corner store in lieu of candy. Sugar was in short supply in those days, the candy counters empty. Coincidentally, the grandfather and the painter lived on the same street. The in-house wakes confused mourners from both wakes and they mingled, discovered their mistakes and left with some measure of embarrassment.

In the year preceding his death, Grandpa had come out of retirement and went back to the ore boat for Bethlehem Steel. The weak heart grew weaker, but the younger men had gone off to the war, so he gave one more year to the war effort. It was his last.

In 1985, Denny would find Grandpa's passport photo in a heap of photos. Years after that, he would find the ship's picture on the internet, the S.S. Josiah G. Munro, later renamed the S.S. Lebanon. Denny wrote a poem about his Mother's Father in 1998 expressing his disappointment in a granddad that went to the lakes in summer and to Florida in the winter, leaving him back in the cold. His other granddad picked up the slack and then some, and filled his heart and his memories forever. His name was Grampa, no 'n,' no 'd.' Grampa.

Grandpa's youngest son went off to the war a merchant marine. Bernard sailed the South Pacific on a liberty ship, keeping the boilers running. His knowledge of photography allowed him to bring home some interesting shots, the bombed out city of Hiroshima, life on a liberty ship, a passing cruiser. Black and white prints, not yet an album, intrigued Denny. Mostly Hiroshima, where a steel frame of some governmental building still stood like a skeletal reminder of the entire city flattened by the first a-bomb. A fruit cake tin full of foreign coins, a silk Japanese flag, and little paper umbrellas made up his collection of memorabilia from his war that saw no blood shed- a fortunate son indeed.

Only the passing cruiser gave a hint of danger to Bernard's war. It was the U.S.S. Indianapolis, a horror story in itself. Denny's ears were filled with it, torpedoed, 700 men in shark infested waters, nobody even searching for them for over a week. Horrible.

The war ended with Denny's dad and brothers up in Canada fishing. They didn't know the war was over until three days later. His life didn't change much except the third grade was smaller than the second. The Jodways moved back to West Virginia. Other kids moved away as the defense plants closed. People took the flags with the stars on them out of the windows. That year, Denny became an altar boy. The world had changed around him, but he didn't see how it had changed in Europe, the Philippines or in the South Pacific. The electric trolley cars got taken away and they paved over the tracks and cobble stones a year later. His older brothers could no longer use a rope to pull the connecting rod off the wire, irritate the conductor and bring the trolley to a halt.

Denny's last recollection of the war occurred in St. Margaret's Church at a Sunday mass. Bernard was home, and in uniform. At some point he removed his handkerchief. Moments later, Denny noticed a wad of money on the floor beneath the pew. As he showed it to Bernard, "Bun, look what I found." Bernard grasped the bundle with both hands, "Oh my God." (He was in church, wasn't he?) Denny got a five dollar reward, a princely sum at the time. Bernard got his back pay for six months. He had no checking account, only a money clip.

Most of all, he remembered when Fleer's bubble gum, Necco Waffers, Hershey bars and that long, twisted, red licorice returned to the corner store. Pepsi, Coke, Dots, Good & Plenty and Butterfingers appeared in unlimited quantities. All you needed was a nickel. No stamps were required for butter or sugar or anything else. Motorists scraped the square gas ration letters from their windshields. The war was over, VJ-Day. Denny was a couple weeks from his eighth birthday.

Necco Waffers------*geeeeez.*

·

Made in the USA
Columbia, SC
07 March 2018